DEAD END TUNNEL

DEAD END TUNNEL

NICK ROBERTS

CONTENTS

.

For Rae & Beth

PART ONE
THE SLEEPOVER

There exists in me a curiosity to examine the past, but then reason steps in and saves me from myself. I've managed to dodge the bullet of recollection for over twenty years now, twenty-four to be precise. But even zeroing in on the exact number gives me pause. Lately, something has been calling me back, beckoning me to remember, and I fear that if I don't do it —don't investigate the dark cave in my mind that's been off-limits for so long—it will metastasize and consume me completely.

On the eve of my thirteenth birthday, my father brought the apocalypse to the dinner table. I vividly recall his statement about the turn of the millennium—that of 1999 to the year 2000 —being the end of civilization as we know it . . . possibly.

What he said confused me at the time, and if I'm being honest, I still don't fully understand what the threat was. When he began to explain that global computer systems could crash because the last two numbers of the digital year had never exceeded 99, my panic subsided. Even if something bad were to happen, it wouldn't be until December, a lifetime away for me at the time.

I was expecting an extinction level event on par with what took out the dinosaurs, not some computer glitch. It wasn't until later in life that I realized how catastrophic the results of what people referred to as "Y2K hysteria" would have been. Worldwide power outages, the collapse of transportation systems, and economic pandemonium would have been the start.

Mom didn't seem as concerned either. She gave Dad the same half-worried look she gave me whenever I scraped my knee or told her I didn't think I did very well on a test—that motherly look that simultaneously told me that she cared, and that there was no underlying danger.

"But do you really think anything will happen?" I remember her asking.

My father, a guidance counselor at the rival middle school I attended, appeared to be considering this, judging by the way his eyes darted back and forth behind his glasses and then stopped abruptly, like he had scanned every possible domino effect in three seconds and said, "No."

Turning my way and speaking in what Mom and I called his "work voice," he said, "How about you, Mav? Have you heard about any of this hoopla?"

Dad's work voice always came out an octave higher than his

"at-home" voice, and his eyebrows went up like they were floating, as if no matter how serious the subject, everything would work out in the end. I knew he talked like that to the students who he said, "didn't have the greatest home life." If my best friend, Max, went to Dad's school, he would fall into that category.

"Yeah," I answered and poked at my Kraft Mac & Cheese.

"Well, what have you heard?"

I took a bite, shook my head, and said, "Just that the world was gonna end."

"Mav, please don't talk with your mouth full," Mom said.

I chewed with my mouth closed.

"How do you feel about that?" Dad asked.

I opened my mouth to respond, but Mom still had her eyes on me and that bite tucked away in my cheek like cow cud.

After three chews and a swallow, I said, "I'm not worried about it if it's just computer stuff."

Dad smiled.

"Yeah, it is," he said and took a drink of his bottled water.

I jabbed as much macaroni as I could fit on my fork and shoveled it in my mouth, chewing as quickly as I could. The green beans were next. Luckily, Mom bought the canned kind. I hated her "fresh" green beans. She must've noticed how fast I ate because she stared at me with that slightly raised eyebrow.

"You're in a hurry, aren't you?"

She knew. I'd been in a hurry all day. It was the night before my birthday. Blake and Max were staying over. We all lived in the same neighborhood, so the plan was for me to ride my bike to each of their houses to round them up. We'd come back to my house and eat pizza and cake, make popcorn, and watch scary movies all night. Whoever fell asleep first would get a

Sharpie mustache at the least, a dick on the forehead if Max held the marker.

I smiled.

"Finished," I said and snatched my empty plate, fork, and cup, darting toward the kitchen sink and left them.

"Excuse me," Mom said.

I knew before she even said it, turning around to put my plate in the dishwasher.

"Thank you," she said from the dining room.

I walked through the other kitchen door and into my room. Looking straight down at my house, you'd see that it was U-shaped, but the round parts were right angles like the top of a field goal post. Practically every house in the neighborhood had this design.

The bottom of the U, the connective part, was where the living room, kitchen, and dining room existed. The kitchen was all the way at the end of the left side, so I had to go through it to enter the beginning of my wing of the house. Well, it wasn't all mine. When you first stepped out of the kitchen, there was a utility room with our washer, dryer, and a large shelving unit that held everything from shoes on the bottom shelf to paper goods and canned food in the middle to my parents' alcohol stash on the top.

The utility room door fed into my room. It was just as big as Mom and Dad's, but that's because it wasn't meant to be a bedroom. With the utility room door to my back, there was a sliding glass door to my right, on the wall directly in front of me at the tip of my U wing, and another one on the left side wall. As if having three sets of sliding glass doors wasn't creepy enough at night, two windows filled the empty spaces on all three walls. It had its own little bathroom between the utility room door and the left wall. My part of the house was clearly meant to be some sort of rec room, but it's where I ended up. If I looked through one of the windows on the right wall of my room, I could see the outside of the other wing across the backyard.

The opposite wing of the house contained my parents' room that had a bathroom built into it, the twins' room directly across the hall from them, and the twins' bathroom closer to the start of the hall. Keep going straight, and you end up back in the dining room.

The twins were gone for the night, though. Looking back on it now, I know that my parents must've orchestrated having them sleep at my cousin's that night because who would want all those kids under one roof at the same time?

The twins, as I called them, hardly ever referring to them individually by their real names, Jill and Jenny, were, to me, one entity. They were four years younger and inseparable. All the weird stuff you hear about twins feeling each other's pain or one finishing the other one's thought is true. It never creeped me out, though, because like I said, they were an it to me.

We used to be a lot closer when I was nine and they were almost five. They looked up to me and let me run the show. Whatever games we played, I dictated the rules, and they followed. We always used my toys, never their Barbies or Cabbage Patch Kids. It was GI Joes and superheroes or nothing.

But then something changed. A little bit after their fifth birthday, they realized they outnumbered me. And worst of all, they didn't need me; they could play with each other. No longer would they have to be subjected to my "boy toys." They could stay in their room and play Barbies. It wasn't that I didn't have my own friends to hang out with at this time, but sometimes I got bored. And the fact that they rebelled against me didn't sit well.

In one last-ditch effort to usurp my status as leader, I walked into their room with my Barbie-sized GI Joe, Snake Eyes. I told them we could play a game where Snake Eyes fought Ken, and that I'd even let Ken win and save the day. They looked at my faux Barbie with disdain. He wore a ninja suit, was jacked like Hulk Hogan, and had a black mask covering everything but his eyes.

"No, thanks," they/it said in unison and went back to having their Barbies shop in the little mall they had created across the carpet.

The words cut me deep. I had lost total control. So vividly I remember that sensation I felt; it was my first time experiencing rejection. In a weird way, they/it were breaking up with me.

I walked over to their stupid mall made of shoe boxes and plastic toy bins and began to kick them all over. They cried and told Mom. I got in trouble, and we never had the same relationship from that point until the day Jenny disappeared shortly after I turned thirteen.

I ran into my room, put my shoes on, and grabbed my fitted Nike hat, making sure to spin it backward before unlocking the left side sliding glass door and stepping onto the stone pathway that ran parallel with the house until making a turn into the driveway.

My Mongoose BMX bike leaned against the basketball hoop with its water-filled base. I grabbed both rubber grips on the handlebar and slung my left leg over, placing my foot on the pedal and pushing down. I kicked off with my right foot and pedaled to the end of the driveway, then cut a sharp right. Once I got going to cruising speed, I sat down, my butt sinking into the gel seat that I'd bought myself.

Max's house was all the way at the end of my street, literally the last house on the left. When we found out there was a horror movie called The Last House on the Left and that it was just about the sickest movie we'd ever seen, Max regularly boasted about the placement of his house. I remember him asking people at school if they'd seen that movie, then telling them that he actually lived in the last house on the left in his neighborhood. From what I recall, nobody but us was impressed.

Our neighborhood, Benson Valley, consisted of two roads: Benson Boulevard and Benson Drive. Benson Boulevard was a circle with houses lining both sides of it and was just a little longer than a mile in circumference. The road that led to town fed into Benson Boulevard, giving us one way in and one way out.

The second road, Benson Drive (mine and Max's road), cut straight through the circle. I always thought our street name got the shit end of the stick. "Boulevard" sounded luxurious, like a property you'd want to buy on Monopoly. "Drive" was boring. There were tons of road names that ended in "Drive" or "Street," but I only knew of one "Boulevard."

I veered left into Max's yard and hopped off my bike before it came to a complete stop. Atop Max's house, the sky had a

7

pink and purple hue that I knew wouldn't last long. Pretty soon it would be dark, and I couldn't wait. I jumped onto the concrete porch and ran to the door. He had a doorbell, but the fake gold knocker that hung in the center just below the small rectangular windows filled me with glee. I grabbed it and gave three good clanks. Max's dog, Vick, barked from the other side, and I heard him running to the door. The old basset hound sniffed and growled. The shadow of his snout darted back and forth in the small crack of light under the door.

"Who is it?" Max's dad, Joel, yelled from, I'm guessing, his dirty old recliner in the living room where he probably sat with his TV dinner resting upon his shirtless beer gut.

Every time I came to Max's after Joel got home, that was where I'd seen him. I knew he wasn't addressing that question to me. He was probably pissed that Max hadn't answered the door yet and Vick was still causing a ruckus.

"Shut up, Vick," I heard Max say as footsteps approached the door.

Max started to open the door, but Joel said, "Where do you think you're goin'?"

Max gave me that annoyed Can you believe I have to deal with this shit? look and yelled back over his shoulder, "It's Mav. I'm staying at his house tonight, remember?"

"You never asked me if you could do that."

"It's for my birthday," I found myself blurting through the crack in the door for no reason.

"I told you last week, Pop. You said it was okay."

We both listened and waited.

"Yeah, whatever," he said. "Don't be a dumbass, though."

"See ya!" Max said and shut the door behind him. "Let's roll."

I picked my bike up from the grass and mounted it as Max

wheeled his from behind the side of the house. He had a Huffy that squeaked and had some rust around the gears. We all knew how much he hated it.

Whenever Blake and I would get a new bike, mostly on birthdays or Christmas, we always showed off to each other, but we tried not to make a big deal about it when Max was around with his old rickety horse. It wasn't his fault Joel wouldn't or couldn't get him a new one. Blake and I hated Joel for that, but we never mentioned it to Max. He would get defensive and actually stick up for his dad. We never understood why. Our best guess was that it had to do with his mom.

Max's mom left him and Joel when he was too young to remember, just up and disappeared on them one day without leaving a note or anything. I couldn't blame her—being stuck in a house with Joel—but she should've taken Max with her, wherever she went. Joel was a trucker and would be gone for days at a time. Sometimes Max would stay with his cousin or me, but mostly he stayed home by himself.

"He doesn't have the greatest home life," Dad had told me on more than one occasion.

"Let's go, fuck-o," he said, riding past me with his black backpack securely strapped to him.

I laughed and followed his lead. Even though his bike was ancient, his ability to ride that thing kept him going at speeds Blake and I couldn't keep up with. Yes, Max "didn't have the greatest home life," but he never let it slow him down.

Immediately after turning left off Benson Drive and onto Benson Boulevard, Max let up, and we rode side by side. He, as was his custom, rode with his arms hanging down at his sides, using his knees to steer. I had no doubt he could ride a unicycle on the first try if he wanted to.

"Tonight is going to be epic," he said.

I stood up and coasted without pedaling, watching the asphalt pass by beneath me.

"Yep," I said, not knowing exactly what he meant by that.

A few minutes later, the sky had already darkened to the point where the bats felt comfortable enough to come out and flap around. It was always fun to get on Blake's trampoline at night with a bunch of pebbles when the bats came out. Jump high enough, toss low enough, and those squeaky little bastards would fly within six inches of your face, mistaking your pebble for a bug.

Blake's house had been a relatively new addition to the neighborhood, as evidenced by it being one of only three two-story homes in Benson Valley. His dad, Walt, worked for the federal government, but Blake wouldn't tell us exactly what he did; I don't even know if he knew at the time. Max and I were convinced that Walt was a G-man, a bona fide FBI agent, but Blake always laughed and shot that theory down.

"My dad doesn't even carry a gun," he would say, as if that closed the case. "Plus, he couldn't fight anybody."

"That's what they want you to think," Max said. "The FBI guys have brains."

The two of us coasted into Blake's freshly paved driveway, an immediate shift from rough asphalt to smoothed-out concrete. We both put our kickstands down. Max's made a metallic whine when he placed it.

"Piece of shit," he muttered.

I pretended to ignore it, never wanting to embarrass him, and began walking along the sidewalk that led to Blake's porch which had five wooden steps and a handrail you had to use to get to the top. He also had a wooden porch swing and two matching rocking chairs.

Blake's mom's ashtray sat on a small table between the

chairs with a few of her Marlboros snubbed out in it. Our theory was that Blake's fed father didn't smoke to stay in shape, and the stress of the job made Blake's mom, Brandy, require some nicotine to steady her nerves at the thought of losing her man on duty.

I rang the doorbell. Blake might've had the better house and more money, but he damn sure didn't have a door knocker, and that scored one major point for Max.

Two locks, one digital, unlocked from the interior. Brandy pulled the door open and smiled at us. She held a glass of red wine in her hand. The inside of Blake's house glowed with the trendy lamps and burning Yankee Candles that smelled like apple pie.

"Hello, boys," she said. "Come on in. Blake is just getting ready."

I could smell the wine on her breath as we stepped into the house. I spotted Walt in the den reading the newspaper with his bare feet propped up on an ottoman. In his gym shorts and white T-shirt, he didn't look like much of a fed. But then again, I found myself second-guessing it when I noticed how ripped the guy was. Not bulky like a bodybuilder, but wiry like Bruce Lee. My conjecture could linger a little longer.

We'd only been in the house for thirty seconds when Blake came running down the stairs.

"Oh, happy birthday, Mav," Brandy said and touched my forearm.

I felt myself flinch down there when her fingers fell against my wrist. At that point in my life, a strong breeze would make my little soldier stand at attention, let alone my friend's hot mom, drunk and getting all touchy-feely.

"Thank you, Mrs. Hirsh," I said, red-faced.

"Y'all ready?" Blake asked as he pulled the second strap of

his backpack over his shoulder and tucked both thumbs underneath.

"Yep," Max said.

"You boys have fun tonight. Blake, call me when you get there so I know you're not pulling one over on me."

Blake gave her a quizzical look.

"I know that old trick," she began. "Blake tells me he's staying with Mav, Mav tells his mom he's staying with Max, Max tells his mom he's staying with Blake, and then you boys get a night to roam wild."

"I don't have a mom, so that plan wouldn't work," Max said with a grin.

I'm sure he was just trying to be witty, but it was obvious that Brandy felt horrible for what she'd just said.

"I'm sorry, honey. I wasn't thinking," she said.

Just then, a cough came from the den. The three of us looked over at Walt as he approached us with his slow, purposeful steps. Somehow his footfalls seemed heavier and louder than a man his size should be capable of producing. We just stared at him in silence. He had brushed back black hair and a matching, neatly trimmed mustache.

He looked at each of us one at a time like he was taking mental pictures. Up until this point, I had had like, three inter-actions with the guy, and his intimidation factor increased with each encounter.

"Happy birthday, young man."

"Thank you . . . sir."

I knew it was polite (and a dying practice) for kids to refer to adults as "sir" or "ma'am," and I certainly never did it, but Walt just brought it out of me. We stood there like we were waiting for him to give us our marching orders.

"I was a teenager, too, once, believe it or not," he said with a hint of a smile that washed away the firm demeanor. "And I did my fair share of tomfoolery in my neighborhood."

"Really? Like what?" Max interjected.

Walt eyeballed Max like he had his WANTED poster hanging up in his study that we were never allowed in, and Max's criminal profile sketched out on a whiteboard.

"Like sneaking out and messing with other people's property," he said to Max and then turned to me. "Or throwing toilet paper in trees or bashing mailboxes. You all aren't going to do anything like that tonight, are you?"

"Of course not," I said.

"No, Dad," Blake said, looking down at the floor, obviously embarrassed and wanting this moment to pass.

"Yeah, definitely not. Messing with people's mail or their mailbox is a federal crime, isn't it?" Max asked, failing to suppress a smile.

"It is," Walt said as he rolled up his newspaper and tapped Max on the shoulder with it. "It's good to know these things. Keeps one out of trouble, you know?"

I could see that whatever look Walt was giving Max worked because that smug smile disappeared from his face, and my friend could only nod his head in agreement.

"Oh, for goodness' sake, Walt, boys will be boys," Brandy said, thankfully stepping in.

She gave Blake a kiss on the cheek that I thought I would've enjoyed more than him, and then she said, "You all have fun. See you tomorrow."

We said our goodbyes and headed to our bikes. Blake had to exit through the garage where he kept his Mongoose. We watched as the door quietly opened, and he walked it out. I saw Brandy press the button inside. She gave me a wave and then disappeared as it shut.

For a moment, we stood there with the front wheels of our bikes all facing each other. Finally, in the darkness of our quiet neighborhood, the three of us were together.

The crickets chirped and an owl hooted in the distance. Every other second a firefly would glow its greenish-yellow light, looking like punctures in the fabric of the dark—holes into a world beyond our world. The warm breeze blew across my skin, and at that point in time, my life was perfect.

As I recall this exact moment, I am tempted to stop now, to end before really beginning. Because if I stop now, in my mind and yours if you're reading this, we could have all lived happily ever after. Nothing bad would've happened. We would've stayed inside my house and ate pizza and watched scary movies and at some point after midnight, I would've turned thirteen years old. We never would've ridden our bikes to that tunnel.

But that's not where the story ends, I'm sad to say. It's where it begins—my part, at least. The darkness we encountered that summer existed long before me. All of this is speculation of course; I can only give my account of what happened before I am consumed by it.

Going to that tunnel on the eve of my birthday wasn't the first mistake we made that night, but for one of us, it turned out to be the last.

PART TWO
THE SLATS

Nights are the worst. When I'm lying in bed, looking at the ceiling but not really seeing it, imagining the abyss that I know exists beyond the stars—the vacuum of space and the coldness for which they don't have words. As my mind travels beyond the planets, the solar system, the galaxy, the ever-expanding universe, what hollows my very being and renders me fetal is that nothingness which dwells within the tears, within the black holes: the absence of existence. It's where light goes to die.

The night before I turned thirteen, Max had been so full of light. We were all on a giddy little high, but Max beamed. It was like he had this hidden agenda or found a treasure map and couldn't wait to show us.

We weaved our bikes between each other down the road that looked like a blacksnake in moonlight. The darkness surrounded us, but strength exists in numbers, and when you've got your two best mates, not even the headless horseman could slow you down.

I caught sight of my porch light. Always having to be the fastest, Max sped up and hit the driveway first. He whipped around and faced us just as Blake and I pulled in. He had that look in his eye like he knew he would always win.

Blake got off his bike, walked it as close to the path beside my house as possible, and rested it on its kickstand. I leaned mine against the house, not bothering with the kickstand, and Max just dropped his on its side like the expendable beast it was.

The three of us hurried to the side door that led to my room. I slid the resistant glass door open, gripping the latch that always stuck with my right hand and pressing my left palm against the glass where I had done it so many times that my handprint was basically embedded in the pane, no matter how much my mom made me Windex it.

"Home, sweet home," Max said, leaping over the back of the couch and landing in a perfectly reclined position in front of the big box TV—my most prized possession—with stacks of VHS tapes unevenly, yet proudly, displayed on both sides.

"Hello, boys," my mom said, using her stealth motherly skills to enter my room without any of us hearing.

Blake and I turned around to see her carrying a small blue gift bag. Max poked his head over the couch.

"Hi, Mrs. Hall," Blake said in that polite tone of his.

"Hey, Mrs. Hall," Max echoed.

She approached me and held out the bag. I grabbed the white ribbon handle and instantly felt the unexpected weight of the bag. I saw the ribbons stretch like they were going to snap and placed one hand on the bottom.

"Don't break it, dude," Max said from behind me, still on the couch.

Mom looked around my shoulder at him.

"Oh, don't worry about that. I think these are pretty indestructible."

That seemed to get Max's attention because in three seconds, he stood at my side, awaiting my opening of the gift. I pulled the white glittery piece of tissue paper out and looked into the bag: three walkie-talkies.

Walkie-talkies? Really?

I quickly forced a smile. Mom knew better.

"You don't like them?"

"What is it?" Max asked.

I grabbed all three by the antennae and pulled them out.

"Oh sweet!" Blake said.

I looked at him, surprised, but not really, because he's into that kind of thing. I mean, he asked for a telescope for Christmas last year. Plus, his possibly-fed dad probably had stuff like this hidden around the house.

"They're not just cheapo Kmart walkie-talkies," she said. "I got them at Radio Shack, and the guy working there assured me that they have a long range, at least a few miles."

Max grinned.

"We could use them around the entire neighborhood," he said.

"That's the idea," Mom said.

Max snatched one out of my hand and began examining its front, back, antenna, knobs. He twisted one, and static buzzed through the speaker. I handed Blake his and kept the last one.

"Well, try it out, Mav," she said.

I turned it on at the same time Blake did.

Max held down the button on the side and spoke into the receiver, "Hello," he said, but we didn't hear anything.

Blake looked down at his, and then at mine, and finally at Max's.

"They're not on the same channel," he said. "Everyone turn to channel one."

We did.

"Testing," Max said, repeating the process, and his voice came through loud and clear this time—a bit too loud, in fact.

After we adjusted our volume levels and began fooling around with them, laughing and saying tame, playful insults, I looked up and saw Mom smiling. She knew we'd like it even though I thought they'd be lame. It never ceased to amaze me how she did this over and over.

Someone knocked on the sliding glass door. It gave me a bit of a startle, but I hid it well. I was glad I did, because my dad stood out there with a grin like he was up to something. He opened the door a lot easier than I did, but it squeaked along the track. His focus shifted from me to the door; his face went from sneaky to concerned.

"Gonna need to get some WD-40 on that thing," he said.

"Worry about it tomorrow, Roger," Mom said/warned.

Dad accepted his orders and focused on the task at hand.

"What are you doing out there?" I asked.

"Admiring the bike collection," he said.

"Mine's the best," Max began. "You can go ahead and say it."

"It's the rider that makes the bike, not the other way around," Dad said and gave Max a wink.

I looked at Max and swore I saw him stand up a little straighter, like he'd never heard a compliment before.

"I have to say, though," Dad began. "Mav, I think yours could use an upgrade."

Just before I opened my mouth to defend myself, I saw that playful gleam in his eye. He was messing with me.

"Did you . . ." I began, but he turned back toward the open door. "Come on out and see for yourself."

I glanced at Mom and smiled. I looked at Max out of habit, hoping to see him share in the revelry with me, but I remembered that he didn't get new bikes. His chest puffed out, though, still holding firmly to what my dad had said.

"Let's go, Mav," Blake said, giving me a nudge on the arm.

Mom smiled and nodded her head.

Wasting no more time and with the walkie-talkie still in my hand, I followed Dad outside. I sped down the path beside the house until I came around the corner to the driveway. The garage door was open, and the light inside gave me a good view of the brand-new bloodred Mongoose BMX bike proudly leaning on its kickstand; however, I got the feeling that this stallion could stand all by itself.

"Holy crap!" I said and ran over to it, looking at every part, touching the reflectors, dragging my hand across the rubber tires that still had that new smell and those tiny rubbery pokeys that would wear off after a few good rides around the neighborhood.

"That is freakin' awesome!" Blake said, walking up behind me.

Max approached us. He squatted down and looked at it the way old men look at muscle cars. I saw that his mouth hung slightly open, and his eyes were full of complete admiration. He'd never reacted so positively to a new bike that Blake or I ever got. Normally, he'd give us a fake good-for-you sign of support, but his jealousy always revealed itself in his eyes. I saw none of that now, though.

"Happy birthday, son."

I turned around and gave him a big hug, then moved on to my mom.

"Thank you," I said. "I love it."

"We figured you could use it with your new walkie-talkies," she said.

I'd completely forgotten that I still held one. I looked down at it.

"Yeah, that'll be cool," I said. "Can we try them out tonight?"

Mom let out a small laugh.

"Not tonight. We'll order pizza for you all in just a little bit and do cake."

Even though I just had dinner about an hour ago, I could always make room for pizza. And then add cake to it? No-brainer.

"I don't really feel like going out anyway," Max said and gave me a wink. "Do you want to go ahead and pick out a movie?"

"Let's do it."

Dad gave me a pat on the back.

"Go ahead and get these bikes wheeled around the side of the house closer to the back. We don't want anyone stealing them."

"Okay."

Dad led Mom into the garage, and just as he pressed the button and the garage door started to move, Mom said, "Happy birthday."

"Thanks, Mom."

As soon as the door closed, I turned to Max.

"What are you planning tonight?" I asked.

"Yeah," Blake jumped in. "I can tell you're wanting to do something . . . shady."

"I've got my own gift for you," Max finally said with a sly grin.

"And what is that?"

"A surprise."

"Well, are you going to give it to me?"

"We have to go get it."

Blake peered at me and then back at Max.

"Where is it?" he asked.

"I can't tell you that. It'd ruin the surprise. Let's just say that we'll need our bikes to get there."

"So we're sneaking out?" I asked, already knowing the answer.

"Well, duh. And then we're going on a little adventure," he said, then put his hand on my shoulder in a rare display of affection that made me just feel awkward. "You're turning thirteen, man. I want to give you something special."

"You're kind of freaking me out right now."

"Dude, you're my best friend," he said and turned to Blake. "Sorry, but he is."

"It's okay," Blake said. "He's my best friend too."

Max nodded his head and looked back at me.

"Are you game?"

"On one condition," I said.

"What?"

"You have to ride my new bike."

Max cocked his head and squinted.

"You want me to ride that?"

"Just tonight. The Red Reaper is all mine after tonight."

I fully expected Max and Blake to laugh at my bike's new name, but they didn't—quite the opposite. They both slowly

21

turned and looked at the bike with what seemed like reverence.

"The Red Reaper," Max said. "You're going to let me ride it first."

"Yeah. You're my best friend too."

I'm still not sure to this day because Max had his back to me when he did this, but he brought his hand up to his face and it looked like he wiped his eyes. It's entirely possible that my gesture had brought a tear to Max's hardened heart. I'm not positive, but I like to believe that to be true.

"Oh cool. I'm second place, I guess," Blake said.

"Shut up," Max teased. "You're rich, and your dad's a badass."

Blake laughed.

"We better get in here and do the birthday stuff," I said.

"Yep. Eat up, fellas. You're going to need your energy."

As the credits rolled on Scream, I glanced at the clock and then at my two friends: Max sitting on the couch beside me and Blake resting in a beanbag in front of the big TV. If that chunky thing were to tip over, Blake would be a pancake.

"It's 11:30," I said.

Blake turned around and looked at us.

"Is it time to go?" he asked.

I looked at Max.

"After Mav's mom comes in to check on us for the last time. They always do that."

He was right. Max was always right. I think he would've

made an excellent police officer or lawyer with his natural ability to read people and predict their behaviors.

"Well, let's speed up the process," I said and stood from the couch.

I turned the overhead lights off. With the TV on the black credits screen, the room got dark real quick. I turned on the small lamp on my homework desk in the corner. Mom could just look out her window across the backyard and see what we were doing if she wanted to. If she saw the lights were off, maybe she'd think we were winding down and come over to say her final good night.

"Put another movie on and kill that one, too," Max said. "We'll just fake like we're asleep when she comes in."

Blake picked out Event Horizon like I knew he would when it was his turn. He loved sci-fi horror. Max and I typically didn't, but Event Horizon had something special to it.

It's about a spaceship that is sent to investigate an SOS beacon from another ship that disappeared years ago. When the salvage team gets there, they discover that the Event Horizon had gone into a different, hellish dimension and reemerged, changed, along with its former crew.

The story, acting, special effects, and especially the gore were all top-notch, and as the cast of characters descends into madness, murder, and mayhem, it just gets darker and darker until its chilling finale.

Looking back on it now, I hate that film. I hate it not because it fails to hold up all these years later; it actually is quite timeless. I hate it because it hits too close to home. I wish I would've seen it that night as the harbinger of doom that it was and not just background noise until my mom came in.

About thirty minutes into the movie, as the crew is boarding the supposedly abandoned spaceship for the first time, I heard my bedroom door open on the other side of the room. We all knew what to do. We'd been preparing for it since the movie started. As soon as my mom entered the room, we shut our eyes and let our heads dangle. Blake made a faint snore that even had me convinced that he was really asleep.

I listened as Mom turned off the TV and stood there, probably just double-checking that we really were all sleeping. A few seconds later, she disappeared from the room. We played it cool for another ten minutes or so until we were sure that she had glanced out her window for the last time and finally gone to bed.

"Y'all ready?" Max asked.

Blake looked at me like he wasn't sure.

"Yep," I answered.

"I guess so," Blake said.

"Okay, ramblers, let's get ramblin'." Max delivered the line exactly like George Clooney did in From Dusk Till Dawn.

With our walkie-talkies in tow, we sped down Benson Drive, the opposite way of Max's house. We were headed toward the exit and onto the "big road." My mom would shit if she knew we left the neighborhood. Forget about just sneaking out at night, that was bad enough, but leaving Benson Valley to ride our bikes on the two-lane road would get me grounded for a month. I guarantee she would've made my dad take that bike back to the store.

Railroad tracks cut across the road which was the only way out of the neighborhood. When a train came through at night, I don't see how the houses near the entrance didn't rattle the residents out of a slumber. But then again, I didn't live that far from the tracks, and it was background noise to me at this point.

The only time the trains really pissed me off was when I

was running late for something, mostly school. I hated being late to school. It also sucked when the weather was hot and Dad refused to roll up the windows, so we all had to just sit there and endure the heat wave and a rhythmic locomotive buffalo stampede until that glorious caboose came into view.

I rode Max's bike instead of my old one just because I was curious to see if I could handle it, and the entire time I thought every screw would pop loose, the wheels would topple sideways, and the handlebars would come off in my hands as I smacked and rolled on the asphalt. It never happened, though. Whatever magic spells Max weaved over his rolling rust bucket worked.

Max kept having to slow down. I knew he would. The Red Reaper would tempt him to unleash its full fury and leave me and Blake in its dust. I struggled to maintain pace with Blake, but my soccer conditioning was paying off. Once we crossed the tracks, the road really got dark. You'd think this stretch would have a few streetlights, but it didn't.

We resided outside of city limits and city maintenance. Getting a hole in the road patched with blacktop was like a birthday present to the grown-ups. The only reason we had some streetlights and pavement in Benson Valley was because of the HOA, about which my parents both bitched and praised, depending on the time of the year and the status of their bank account.

The "big road" was a mile-and-a-half stretch of country back road that ran along the winding river, matching its bending shape when needed. In the final stretch, you had to ride through a C-shaped turn before it finally ended at the tunnel.

Broadside Road, the real "big road," began city limits, had two freshly painted lanes, and led straight to downtown

Franklin with bystreets of other neighborhoods branching off it. These were destinations normally reached only by automobiles. The three of us were certainly not allowed to ride to the tunnel—day or night—but the idea of taking a bicycle through the tunnel and onto Broadside was approaching punishments that read more like prison sentences if we got caught.

Turning thirteen sent little clumps of the rational decision-making part of my brain down to my balls and gave me a bad case of the fuck-its. Somehow, Max's idea of riding not just to the tunnel, but through it, and then going half a mile down Broadside Road to our closest convenience store, 7-Eleven, seemed like the thrill my soul craved that night.

When he proposed his plan to go to 7-Eleven and bribe the night worker, Harley, to sell us a pack of cigarettes and a twelve-pack of beer, Blake, as predicted, balked. He wanted to know why and then stammered out all the things that could go wrong and the terrible consequences his parents would bestow on him. None of us had drunk alcohol. According to Max, he had smoked one of his dad's cigarettes and said it made him sick, but "only because he didn't do it right."

My instinct was to agree with Blake, but it wasn't until Max revealed that he'd been saving what little allowance Joel had given him just to provide me with this life experience for my birthday, that I finally consented. I'm pretty sure Blake noticed how much this meant to Max because even his initial refusal didn't last long. He, too, knew how scarce money was for Max. Looking back on it now, Max technically gave me a present, but by us going with him, allowing him to be the ringleader/expedition guide on this daring journey, I knew we were really the ones giving him the gift.

We cruised along that dark and windy road with no problem. No cars even passed us, which was always a source of worry because if one of those drivers noticed three teenage boys riding on the "big road" this late at night, they might tell our parents. Everyone in Benson Valley knew everybody.

Max hit the brakes and turned his/my bike sideways at the mouth of the tunnel. Blake and I pedaled up to him and planted our feet on the road. I stared at the giant black arch. It would be cliché to compare it to a gaping mouth, but in my mind, that's what it was. Calling it anything but that would be disingenuous. I'd never been scared of it until that moment.

The river snaked off to the left at this point to feed into a bigger river. The riverbank turned into a gradual hill that quickly became a steep incline of trees and stone covering the tunnel. This hill seemed to go up and up until it finally leveled off somewhere out of sight. A neighborhood supposedly existed up there, but we couldn't see it from the road. We only saw the tunnel that burrowed through the earth and the giant boulders protruding from the mountainside.

I looked at the CAUTION: FALLING ROCK sign on the right side of the road. It had been there for as long as I could remember, yet I'd never seen so much as a pebble roll down the hill. There was this one big rock that looked like a flying saucer made out of stone trying to escape the mountain. I always wondered if that was what the sign was referring to.

Any time I'd be in the car waiting to go through the tunnel and that rock would catch my eye, I'd imagine it finally snapping, finally breaking loose, and coming crashing down the hill, destroying everything in its wake before eventually landing on me.

Staring up at it in the darkness made it no less intimidating. I saw its silhouette in the moonlight. If it fell now, we'd all be goners.

"Nothing's coming," Blake said.

He was referring to the fact that no cars were currently driving through the tunnel. Back then, it didn't have traffic lights. Right before the CAUTION: FALLING ROCK sign stood a red STOP sign. The idea was that cars would wait, and the drivers would lower their windows and turn down their radios as they listened for the honking of other drivers. If there was no sound, you honked your horn, waited a moment, turned on your headlights whether it was day or night, and then slowly drove through the darkness, honking every few seconds to prevent anyone on the other side from coming.

It wasn't the best system in the world, but it worked for the most part. In doing my research years later on car crash fatalities within the tunnel, I found fewer than a dozen, and most of them were either teenagers not obeying the proper protocol, drunk drivers, or elderly people.

That was the danger of going through in a car.

We were about to take our chances on bikes. Not only did we not have horns to blow if we saw the headlights of an oncoming automobile, but we'd have to somehow wedge ourselves against the wall and pray that the driver wouldn't run us over.

"You all ready?" Max asked.

"What do we do if a car comes?" I asked, trying not to sound scared.

"The slats," Blake said.

"Huh?"

"Yeah," Max said, clearly picking up on something that I wasn't. "If a car comes, we lean our handlebars into the slats and squeeze in. We'll be perfectly flush with the wall."

"Oh yeah," I said, still nervous but seeing the logic in their plan. "I never really thought about that."

The wooden tunnel had an arch shape, and every couple of

yards, a new support arch would stretch from one side of the road up and over to the other side. It was between these arches that would be our sanctuary should we encounter a vehicle.

"It's late, though. I don't even think anyone's coming through there. We haven't seen a car yet," Max said.

"All right," I said and began to pedal. "Let's go."

Max had to pick up the front of his/my bike to prevent me from running into the wheel.

"Last one through stays stuck forever!" I shouted, suddenly feeling the rush of adrenaline as I pedaled into the pitch-black pathway.

"Oh, screw that. I'm smokin' all of you," Max said from behind me.

I heard them laughing and pedaling as they gained on me. A grin crept across my face, but it was too dark for anyone to see it. The soundtrack of our race echoed ahead of us.

I was so fully present. The thing about adrenaline is that it forces you to be fully in the moment, one hundred percent. I wasn't thinking about anything else other than making it to the other end of that tunnel.

"You're not going to beat me, fuck-o," Max said, now right beside me, but I still couldn't see him.

"Make way!" Blake said from the other side of me.

I realized how dangerous it was for the three of us to be racing side by side in a one-lane tunnel, especially one with a bend in the middle. If you could cut the mountain off the top of the tunnel and look down, it would be shaped like the letter C. A single wrong move and someone's outside handlebar would hit one of those slats, and we'd all be playing Slip 'N Slide on the asphalt.

And that's when I saw the bright headlights appear around the curve.

They made me squint at first, then became blinding when the driver turned on the high beams. I saw Max to my left just ahead of me and Blake a little behind on my right. If that light was a camera's flashbulb taking a snapshot of the end of a race, Max would've gotten the gold, I would've claimed silver, and Blake would've earned the bronze.

I did the only thing I knew to do and squeezed my handlebar brakes. As soon as Max passed me, I swerved into the now empty space on my left. The car honked its horn, sending a deafening echo throughout the enclosed tunnel. I planted both feet on the ground and leaned into the slats.

Across the road, Blake did the same thing. The car blared its horn again. I couldn't see Max. To do that, I'd have to stick my head out of the protective confines of the slats and risk decapitation. All I could do, in all my cowardice, was bury my face into the tunnel wall and close my eyes until the car zipped by me, never slowing as it disappeared into the night, leaving us once again in complete darkness.

I peeled myself from the cool wood and wiped specks of dirt off my face.

"Mav, are you okay?" Blake asked from the other side of the road.

"Yeah. Holy shit. We almost died," I said. "Max, are you good?"

There was no response.

"Max?" Blake called.

I heard the fear bubbling in his tone. Neither of us could see six inches in front of our faces. For all we knew, Max was a smear on the asphalt. A sick feeling formed in the pit of my stomach.

"Just leave your bike and walk," I said as I got off mine and hurried forward, careful to keep my left hand running along the wall and slat, wall and slat, wall and slat.

If Max had pulled off on my side like he should have, I would've bumped into him by now.

But there was nothing, not even his bike . . . my bike.

"Max!" Blake yelled. "If you're joking, this isn't funny!"

I'd never heard Blake mad like that, but it really wasn't anger, was it? He was scared, just like me.

"Do you feel anything over there?" I asked.

"No."

"Just keep walking forward."

"What do you think I'm doing?"

We moved through the darkness until moonlight from the other side of the tunnel came into view. We kept walking and never ran into him. I saw the fear in Blake's wide eyes.

"Where is he?" he asked.

"I don't know. Did you hear . . . anything?"

"Anything like what?"

"You know," I began, not wanting to say it. "Him getting hit by that car."

"No. I was in the same tunnel you were."

I quickly surmised that Blake turned into a major dick when he was scared.

"We gotta go back," I said. "He's either in there hurt or messing with us. You know, I didn't hear anything either. It wouldn't surprise me if he turned around and rode after the car when we still had our heads turned."

I could tell by his face that he wasn't a fan of my theory.

"All right," he said and went back into the tunnel.

We trudged through, using our hands to navigate our way. Something hard banged into my shin.

"Ouch! Shit!" I said and hopped on one leg for a second.

31

"Is it him?" Blake asked.

I reached down and felt the bike. Just by feeling the loose rubber grips on the handlebars, I knew it was Max's bike, the one I'd been riding.

"I found mine, too," Blake said.

I listened to him pick it up and heard the spokes as he began to push it.

"Let's see if he's out here," he said.

I walked Max's bike back through the tunnel. The both of us covered every inch as we retraced our steps, but there was no sign of him or my new bike. When we emerged through the other end, headed back to Benson Valley, we laid our bikes down and continued to yell for our missing friend.

"This doesn't make sense," I said. "He couldn't just disappear in the middle of the tunnel. He had my bike. How are they both gone?"

Blake didn't answer my question.

"That's not all he had," he said.

"What are you talking about?"

Blake unclipped his walkie-talkie from his belt. I immediately fumbled for mine which was in the front pocket of my jean shorts. We both turned them on at the same time. Static hissed until Blake held down the button to speak and said, "Max? Come in, Max."

He released the button and the static resumed. We listened for a voice we knew wasn't coming. The crickets and tree frogs made louder pleas than anything that came from that speaker. I brought my walkie-talkie to my mouth.

"Max, it's Mav. Can you hear us? If you're messing with us, we give up. You got us. We're worried, man."

Still nothing but the quiet hum of hollow noise.

Blake sighed and turned off his walkie-talkie.

"We have to go home and tell our parents."

He was right. At this point, I didn't care about getting in trouble. I just wanted to know that Max was okay, and if he wasn't, then it was doubly important that we found him. I turned the volume down and put the walkie-talkie back into my pocket.

"Okay," I said. "Come on. Let's go."

The two of us mounted our bikes and pedaled toward Benson Valley. Just as the train tracks came into view, I heard a faint, muffled voice say, "Mav?"

My heart froze. I stopped the bike in the middle of the road and listened, my ears instinctually pricked up. Blake saw me, and he stopped too.

"What are you doing?" he asked, pedaling back to me.

"Shh," I said, cutting him off.

The low sound of white noise was coming from my pocket. I reached in and withdrew the walkie-talkie that I hadn't completely turned off. Blake put his feet on the ground and stared at me. I slowly turned the volume knob, and the sound of static intensified. We waited and stared, and just when I was about to cut it off, a voice whispered, "Help."

PART THREE
THE AFTERMATH

The night Max disappeared in the tunnel in the summer of 1999 changed the lives of an entire neighborhood and beyond, the scope of which I'll never be entirely sure. But as I sit here and write this, knowing what I know now and reliving every detail of that night, it's easy to see why Joel did what he did.

Every action has a reaction. Each reaction has another reaction. One event has the capacity to exponentially alter the world. Call it a chain reaction, a domino effect, a butterfly effect, etc. Throw the label on it that best enables your understanding, but in the end, it doesn't matter.

It's all just chaos.

Standing on our bikes at the entrance to Benson Valley, Blake and I stared at the walkie-talkie in my hand.

"You heard that, right?" I asked.

Blake could only nod his head, unable to break eye contact with the device. I pulled it close to my mouth and pressed the button to talk.

"Max?"

We waited, listening to the static that seemed to drone on forever. Thinking back on it now, as awful as it is to admit, I didn't want my suspicions confirmed. I didn't want Max's disembodied voice to come from my walkie-talkie and ask for help. If he was gone, I wanted him gone.

I didn't want to have to deal with an ongoing situation. I wanted to live my life. That's how I felt in those moments of static, but as soon as I heard Max's voice again, all I wanted was my friend back.

"... Mav? ... Mav, is that you?"

Blake, still sitting on his bike seat, quickly wheeled up beside me.

"Yeah, Max. Me and Blake are here. We're at the tracks. Where are you?"

"... You're ... at the tracks? ... What tracks? ... I don't see any tracks, Mav ..."

Blake and I shared bewildered expressions, and then he fumbled for his device but came up short.

"I think I dropped mine. Can I see it?" Blake whispered for some reason, and I handed him my walkie-talkie. "Max, it's Blake. What do you see? Tell us exactly what you see."

"... See?"

A long hiss of static lingered and then desperate laughter came through.

"... There's nothing to see ... It's just ... empty."

"Wait, are you inside the tunnel?" Blake asked as his eyes darted back and forth.

"... Guys, there's something else here now ..."

I snatched the walkie-talkie back and spoke, "What is it, Max?"

"... It's looking at me ..." he whispered. " ... I can see its eyes. I think it sees me. Oh shit. It definitely sees me. Oh shit!"

"Max!"

"................"

And then it was nothing but static, and we were both staring at a useless Radio Shack walkie-talkie.

"We have to go back!" I cried, turning my bike around as I spoke.

"What? Are you serious?"

I turned to face him. "Come on! We have to help him!"

"Mav, it'll take us forever to get back there. Let's go to your house and wake your parents up. We can't do anything about this."

It tore at me, but I knew he was right. Wasting no time debating myself, I huffed and whipped my bike back around and pedaled toward the tracks with Blake close behind.

We went to my house because it was closest and woke my parents up to tell them about what happened. Dad kept asking us the same questions over and over again, no matter how many times we told him we were positive that Max hadn't been hit by the car or abducted. No, we couldn't find his bike. No, he wasn't playing a practical joke on us. This was for real. We knew he was in danger. He'd cried for help on the walkie-talkies!

The whole time Dad talked to us, I could hear Mom in the kitchen fumbling with the telephone that hung on the wall.

"Joel didn't answer," she said from the other room.

"Of course he didn't," Dad muttered, then looked up at us like he immediately regretted saying that out loud.

I heard Mom pick the phone back up and even the faint dings of her pressing the numbered buttons.

"Hello, Walt?" I heard her say.

Blake looked at me, wide-eyed and pale-faced, as if the fact that his parents were now involved made all this real, or at least threw some culpability his way.

"We need to be calling the cops!" I finally snapped. "He could seriously be hurt right now. You all didn't hear him on the walkie-talkie. I did."

"Calm down, son," Dad said. "We're handling it. You want to hear what's on the walkie-talkie right now?"

He got up, walked into the kitchen, and returned with the walkie-talkie that was still hissing.

"We've had it on since you gave it to us. There's nothing there."

Before I could scream Bullshit! to my dad for the first time, he said, "Mav, trust me."

I nodded my head. He took it back to the kitchen where my mom was.

Less than ten minutes after that, our doorbell rang and Walt and Brandy Singer hurried inside; Brandy wearing pajama pants and a matching top, and Walt still wearing the gym shorts and white T-shirt from earlier. After getting the same round of questioning from Brandy, Walt led my father to a corner of the living room. I couldn't hear what they were talking about, but

Dad kept looking back at me as if to make sure I wasn't hearing them.

"I'm going to try Joel again," Mom said and walked into the kitchen.

She must've called repeatedly, judging by how many times I heard her pick up and hang up the phone receiver. She stormed back into the living room.

"I'm just driving down there. I'll pour a bucket of water on his face if that's what it takes to wake him from his stupor. His child is missing, and he's piss-drunk and passed out," she said.

I'd never heard my mom say that expression before.

"Leah," Dad said as she put her slippers on and grabbed her purse from the closet beside the front door.

"He needs to be here," she said.

"Leah," came a stern voice from the corner.

Mom stopped and turned around. Blake and I had been watching her, so we followed her gaze. Walt had stepped forward and stared at my mom like a gunslinger who'd just called someone out for a duel.

"Don't," he said.

Mom took a few angry breaths and looked at Dad. He nodded. I had no idea what was going on. Why Blake's dad was running this show like he'd been in similar scenarios before. But then it was so obvious, wasn't it? Blake's dad, Walt, the fed, was finally revealing his true colors to us. I looked at Blake, but he still stared at his father.

"We're going to call the sheriff's department," Walt said. "That's step number one. We'll let them deal with Joel."

"But what if Max is home with Joel?" Mom asked. "Shouldn't we rule that out before—"

"The police will sort it out," Walt asserted.

"Walter," Brandy said, touching her husband's arm.

39

He looked into her eyes, and that's all it took for him. The tenseness in his face relaxed, and he took a breath and then looked back at Mom.

"I'll call nine-one-one," Mom said and headed back to the kitchen.

Surprisingly, it didn't take long for the deputy sheriff on duty to arrive. His tall frame and hat forced him to hunch under the arched entrance to the living room.

"Hello. I'm Sheriff Potts," he said and placed his hands on his hips.

All the parents introduced themselves.

Sheriff Potts nodded and said, "I just wanted you all to know that there are two men at the tunnel now. We've got it temporarily shut down."

"Boys," my dad said, and we both switched from Sheriff Potts to him. "Tell the sheriff exactly what you told us."

I looked at Blake just as he did me. His eyes were pleading for him to not have to do it. I felt my heartbeat increase and my hands getting clammy.

Max's smiling face appeared in my mind as he rode the Red Reaper toward the tunnel and skidded the back wheel around in that really cool way that only he could do, and I found the courage to open my mouth.

"We snuck out a little after midnight because we were riding to 7-Eleven. It's my birthday, and Max wanted to buy me a bunch of candy," I said, omitting the beer and cigarettes plan. "We rode our bikes out of the neighborhood and to the tunnel."

I felt my heart start to beat even faster as I recalled being in there.

"We made sure no cars were coming, and we had a plan to move out of the way and lean into the slats, like this, if a car did come through, but we didn't think anybody would be out that late anyway."

"Okay," Sheriff Potts said. "Now tell me exactly what happened in the tunnel."

"Well, it was pitch black. We all know how the tunnel is shaped, and once you ride around that one bend you can see the other side, so we weren't scared to go through it.

"I was the first one to ride in. Max was behind me on the left and Blake was behind me on the right. We started to race, and Max got a little bit ahead of me, and that's when the car came out of nowhere. They didn't stop and honk or flash their lights from the other side like they were supposed to. If they had, none of this would've happened."

"Okay, pause right there and tell me every detail about what happened next."

I told him how the car came around the curve, and we hid in the slats. I told him how I saw Blake do exactly what I did because he was across the tunnel from me, and I could see him in the headlights. Max was farther ahead of me, though, and I was too scared to look forward because I didn't want to get hit.

"Did you see what color the car was? Better yet, did you happen to get a license plate number or anything like that?"

I looked at him like he hadn't heard a thing I'd said.

"I couldn't even look. I closed my eyes and hid in that little spot until it was quiet. I didn't even look up until way after the car was gone."

"I see," he said and then looked at Blake. "How about you, son? Did you see anything?"

"The car was red. I could tell that much," he said. "Red like blood . . . like the color of Mav's new bike."

This was news to me. The sheriff waited for him to elaborate.

"I saw it drive out, but I didn't look at the license plate. And I didn't see what happened to Max. We searched for him, though. We walked from one side of that tunnel to the other, and he wasn't there. His bike wasn't even there. Well, Mav's bike. Mav let him ride his new bike."

"He is still in there, though," I interjected.

My dad sighed like he was embarrassed about what I was about to say.

"And how do you know that?" the sheriff asked.

"The walkie-talkies."

"What walkie-talkies?"

My dad stepped toward us.

"We got Mav these three walkie-talkies for his birthday, which they took with them."

The sheriff looked at my dad. His interest was piqued.

"And where are they now? Can you get them for me?"

"We only have the one," I said. "Max had the other one, and Blake dropped his along the road."

"I'll get it," Mom said and walked into the kitchen, returning almost immediately with my walkie-talkie in hand, still hissing. "Here you go."

She handed it to the sheriff.

"Have you had this on the whole time they've been back here?"

"Yes," Dad said.

The sheriff turned the knob louder and held the button down to speak.

"Hello, this is Sheriff Potts with Hillsbury Sheriff's Department. I'm trying to reach Max McNeil. Max, if you can hear me, please respond."

Sheriff Potts held the walkie-talkie away from his face, almost in the middle of us so that we could all hear. I looked around at everyone doing the same thing: leaning in, listening for any sign of life.

But nothing came.

Sheriff Potts waited a full minute before trying again— saying the exact same thing—and again, we listened and waited. After another minute, he spoke into the walkie-talkie again, but this time, he said something that made my eyes widen.

"If Max McNeil is in someone's custody against his will, it would be in your best interest to respond to me right now."

No one breathed as we all stared at the staticky walkie-talkie.

The front door burst open, and we all jumped back. I noticed Sheriff Potts's hand unstrap his holstered pistol in a split second, but he didn't draw it.

"Where is he?" an angry, middle-aged man hollered from the entryway.

The wall separating our room from the front door shielded the view of the intruder until he took a few more steps into the opening that led to the living room.

"Where's my son?" Joel asked, stumbling forward and looking at us all one by one until he saw my mom. "I got your message on the machine. Where is he?"

"Sir, calm down," Sheriff Potts said, standing between Joel and Mom. "Are you Max McNeil's father?"

"Where's Max?" Joel asked, looking the sheriff dead in the eyes.

"Calm down."

"Don't you tell me to calm down until you tell me where my fucking son is!" Joel said as he pointed his finger in the sheriff's face.

Sherriff Potts didn't move.

Mom and Brandy stood by the fireplace and just watched. Dad was behind Sheriff Potts, but not like he was backing him up or anything. He was watching everything unfold along with everyone else.

Walt stepped in between the sheriff and Joel and placed his hand on Joel's shoulder. Joel swung his head like he was about to beat the pants off whoever just touched him, but once he saw Walt standing there, he lost the fire in his eyes.

"The boys snuck out," Walt said, speaking directly to Joel.

Joel kept breathing quick, adrenaline-fueled breaths, almost panting like a dog, but he listened as Walt continued.

"They were riding their bikes to 7-Eleven, and there was some kind of incident."

Joel's eyes turned from fury to fear as his mind appeared to be contemplating something.

"Where was the incident?"

Walt didn't say anything.

"Walt, where was the incident?"

Walt looked down at the floor, breaking eye contact.

"The tunnel," Walt finally said.

Joel's jaw dropped and he stumbled backward until he hit the wall. Tears quickly formed in his eyes and dribbled down his cheeks.

"No, God, no," he cried, looking around the room hysterically.

I didn't know why he was acting like this at the time. Walt didn't tell him what kind of incident or even where Max was. I looked around the room, and the only people who seemed perplexed by this reaction were Blake, Sheriff Potts, and me. The other adults in the room just shared this knowing glance that jumped from person to person.

Joel slid down the wall and cupped his face in his hands. My mom and Brandy finally sprang into action and rushed to his side, telling him the standard things you're supposed to tell someone in a situation like this.

"It'll be okay."

"Don't assume the worst."

"We'll figure this out."

Walt turned to face the sheriff.

"I need you to let me know exactly what's going on here. Time to level with me," the sheriff said.

Walt nodded and began to speak in a hushed tone, making sure his back was to Joel.

"His wife left him a few months after Max was born."

I looked sideways at Blake—careful not to move too much and cause Walt to stop talking—to see if Blake was listening to this inside scoop as well, which he was. We sat quietly as Walt continued.

"She wasn't well, Darla, his wife. Suffered a bad case of postpartum depression. She was close to my wife," Walt said with a flick of his head, gesturing toward Brandy who was still behind him comforting Joel. "Anyway, she left him a few months after Max was born. No note, no nothing. Just left most of her stuff and hauled out while he was working."

"What's this got to do with the current situation?" Sheriff Potts interjected.

Walt bit his lip and shook his head like he didn't want to say what he was about to say.

"Because he thinks the tunnel took her," he finally said.

Sheriff Potts's face slowly screwed into a look of befuddlement, and Walt nodded his head as if acknowledging how crazy it sounded.

"But why—" Sheriff Potts began but cut himself off when Joel started to get off the floor.

"I'm all right," Joel said to the two women as he dried his face and looked around the room.

I quickly looked away before I could match his gaze. I didn't want him to see me seeing him like that.

Walt made room for Joel between him and Sheriff Potts. Dad was still standing near the far end of the couch, closer to us than the other adults. I looked at him with his arms crossed, seemingly unaffected by the events unfolding in his living room this late at night or early in the morning, depending on how you looked at it.

"So, what happened?" Joel asked the sheriff.

Sheriff Potts had a small notepad and pen in his hand and glanced down at it as he began to speak, "According to the other boys, the three of them entered the tunnel and a car came through. Maverick—"

"Mav," I said, interrupting the sheriff.

My dad shot me a look quicker than the sheriff could shoot his pistol, but I didn't care. I hated when people called me by my full name. The sheriff glared at me and then back at his pad.

"Mav was the first one to enter the tunnel, and Max and Blake followed him in. The car allegedly ignored the standard procedures of stopping and honking before entering the tunnel on the opposite end. The car came through as the boys were coming around the curve. Mav and Blake got off their bikes and positioned themselves in the slats of the tunnel as the car passed. Neither boy could account for Max's actions as they stated that they couldn't see him at the time. The car exited the tunnel. The boys searched the tunnel but found no sign of Max or his bicycle. They returned here to this premises, informed Mr. and Mrs. Hall about what happened, and then they called it in."

Sheriff Potts folded his pad and looked around.

"Did I get everything?" he asked.

Blake and I nodded.

"Has anyone been to the tunnel?" Joel asked, his voice a pathetic whimper.

"I have two men there right now, as I explained to everyone before you showed up, Mr. McNeil."

"I'm going over there," Joel said and wiped his face. "It's no fuckin' use, but I'm going."

He turned around and started to head out the way he came in.

"Mr. McNeil," Sheriff Potts said in a tone that made him stop and turn around.

"You've been . . ." The sheriff looked at us and then back to Joel. "You're in no shape to drive. I've got what I need here for now. You can ride with me."

"The hell I will," Joel said and resumed his exit.

"Joel, I'll take you," Walt said and walked around the sheriff, grabbing Joel by the arm.

"Fine, whatever," I heard Joel say as the two men disappeared from the house.

"I want to go," I said.

"No!" my dad blared from over my shoulder, causing me to jump. "You've done enough for one night, wouldn't you say?"

His face had the complexion of a ripe tomato.

"I—"

"I don't want to hear anything from you," he said, cutting me off. "Go to your room and get some sleep."

"Sleep? I can't sleep with this—"

"I didn't ask!"

I'd never seen my dad so angry. Had I not just turned into a teenager hours before, I probably would've cried. I immediately got up and stormed out of the living room. When I got to the kitchen, I heard Brandy tell Blake that she was taking him home, too, and he was in deep trouble. As I passed the refrigerator on my right, I noticed something on the kitchen table to my left: the walkie-talkie.

Without thinking, I snatched it and opened the door to the utility room, passed through there, and entered my room, slamming the door behind me. I hurried over to my bed, not bothering to turn on any lights. As I looked out all of the windows I saw the sky was lightening, and sunrise wasn't far off.

Cradling the walkie-talkie like it was contraband, I tucked it under one of my blue pillows that matched the Dallas Cowboys comforter on my bed. Right before I pulled the covers back to climb in, I realized how sweaty and dirty my clothes were. There were still splinters of wood from the tunnel slats embedded in my shorts and shirt like thorns.

I stripped down to my underwear and climbed in bed. Taking a shower could wait until later. I took the walkie-talkie back out from under the pillow and turned it up. The sound of static filled the large, quiet room. My heart pounded at the thought of what I was about to do, but I didn't know how long I would have the device in my possession. Any minute now, the sheriff or my mom and dad could come busting in here and take it from me. It was now or never. I brought it up to my face and pressed the <TALK> button.

"Max? Come in, Max," I whispered. "It's Mav."

"..............."

I watched through the sliding glass door that led to the

driveway and saw headlights receding and moving along the side of the neighbor's house. Brandy must be taking Blake back to his house. That meant Mom and Dad would probably come and check on me any minute now.

"Max, are you in the tunnel?"

". . . . ."

"Please, Max. Just answer. They're going to take the walkie-talkie away when they see that it's missing . . ."

". . . Mav?"

I lurched up in bed.

"Max, it's me. Are you okay?"

". . . Yeah, Mav . . . I'm okay . . ."

"Where are you? You have to come home. The freakin' police are involved, man!"

". . . . ."

"Max? Max, are you still there? Did you hear me?"

". . . I know . . . I can see them . . ."

"What do you mean you can see them?"

". . .There's two cops walking around with flashlights. There are blue and red lights and headlights from the cops' cars . . . It's so . . . pretty . . . It's the redness, Mav. The redness . . ."

"Max, call for help! You're not in trouble. I promise!"

". . . Hey, there's my dad . . . and Blake's dad . . . Are they looking for me too?"

"Yes! Everyone is. How can you see all of them and they can't see you?"

". . . I'm in . . . the dark place, Mav . . ."

I just held my walkie-talkie, not having a clue what to say to that.

". . . But guess what?"

"What?"

". . . My mom is here, Mav . . ."

49

My heart skipped a beat. If Max's mom wasn't dead, she'd been missing his whole life. And after what Walt said about Joel thinking the tunnel "took her," I was beginning to sweat all over.

"...I can see her ... She's just trapped, is all ..."

"Max, just yell. Please. Just start screaming so someone will find you," I said and started to weep. "Please."

"...You don't need to cry, Mav. You know why?"

"Why?"

"...Because he's going to ... let me go ..."

"What are you talking about? Who is going to let you go?"

"...Tomorrow night ... He's letting me go tomorrow night . .. and I'll come and see you ..."

PART FOUR
THE RETURN

In trying to explain the unexplainable, one of two things will happen: revelation or insanity. The insidiousness of it all is that you won't know which one you've attained. When people go mad, they don't feel like they're losing their grip on reality; they feel it strengthening. You will not hear a person tumbling down the mountains of madness say, "I think I'm going crazy."

Ironically, when you do feel like you're going off the rails, the barometer of your mental faculties is finely tuned and operating as designed. It's your body's natural warning system against lunacy—an emergency broadcasting channel buried deep within your gray matter that's trying to course correct. When you feel like you're becoming enlightened and everyone else is losing their shit, it's too late.

I've managed to hold it together all these years through sheer avoidance. Until recently, the events that happened that summer were nothing more than an old movie I watched once and put back on the shelf to collect dust. The problem is that now, for reasons I've yet to comprehend, the film plays on repeat in my head. The tunnel wants me to remember. I have no choice now. I can no longer pretend it didn't happen. And the bitch of it is that I'll never truly know which one will take the cerebral cake: revelation or insanity.

The search for Max lasted all night and into the next day. I slept in too long. It wasn't by choice; I was exhausted. That's not entirely true, though. After Max had said he'd come to see me the next night, I kept asking him how he was going to do that, but I never got a reply. I remember just sort of lying there, staring at the dark ceiling until my mind and body called it quits in unison.

I woke up a little after noon. I opened my eyes and saw the sunrays blaring through the windows on the eastern wall. I scrunched up my face, pulled the covers over my head, and rolled in one efficient twist. Just as I managed to achieve enough of a shield to go back to sleep, the events of the previous night flooded back like a movie on fast-forward.

Holy shit!

I threw the covers off me and stumbled out of bed, my right foot getting caught in the comforter, causing me to land on my chest against the floor. There's nothing like the rush of falling and having the wind knocked out of you to wake you up. Regaining my composure, I threw on a pair of gym shorts and a T-shirt and ran to tell my parents about what had happened once I'd been sent to my room.

The kitchen was empty. I ran into the living room, expecting to see a ragtag band of searchers, but only saw an empty couch and chairs.

Where is everybody?

I hurried across the bottom part of the horseshoe shape of our house and into the hallway where my sisters' and parents' rooms stood.

"Mom? Dad?"

No response, only silence.

As I stood there, staring down the empty hallway which now looked like a long and desolate corridor, I felt an overwhelming sense of dread in my chest, and I found it hard to breathe. This was my house, but I felt something lurking beneath its façade. I felt like I was dreaming but knew I wasn't. As quickly as the panic set in, it dissipated. The hallway was just a hallway once again, one I'd walked, ran, marched, and crawled across several times. I took a deep breath and moved forward.

Jenny and Jill's room remained the same as it had since they'd left to go stay with our cousins yesterday afternoon. I walked a little farther and looked into Mom and Dad's room. The king-size bed had been made. Aside from a pile of Dad's folded clothes on their dresser (which Mom would have him put away before the day ended, I was sure), everything had been tidied up.

Maybe I missed a note?

I hurried back to the kitchen. We had a small dry-erase board that clung to the refrigerator by four magnets. It mostly functioned as a grocery list or a reminder to do chores and homework, but today, written in my mom's cursive handwriting, the note read Went to get your sisters and pick up Burger King. Be back shortly. Love, Mom.

"Burger King?"

On top of eating something from my least favorite fast-food joint, I was now coming to terms with the fact that I'd soon have to be around the twins while all of this was going on. Before I could go on a long-winded mental rant, perspective snuck up behind me, tapped me on the shoulder, and back-handed me, as it often does. The cold, hard fact was that my best friend had gone missing the night before, and I still managed to make it all about me and my troubles.

The garage door hummed its mechanical groan just as I grabbed a can of Mountain Dew, my mind and body needing all the caffeine I could get.

They're home! How do I tell them about what happened without sounding crazy? Dad would probably start in with his half-assed school counselor rationalizations. Or maybe not. Maybe this new intel on the walkie-talkie is just what they need. Dad might not know what to do with it, but maybe Walt or Sheriff Potts would.

Even then, I knew there was more to this than they were letting on.

The door from the garage to the utility room opened, and my sisters bounded into the kitchen, each one carrying a different Disney princess backpack and their chosen American Girl dolls. I never saw the appeal in those damn things, and it wasn't until I got older that I realized the small fortune my parents must've doled out in buying not just two dolls, but the accompanying books, different outfits, and other accessories.

"Hi," I said, just now hearing the croak in my voice. I sipped my Mountain Dew. "Did you all have fun?"

They said, "Fine," at the same time and zipped past me.

I stepped to my right to get a good look down the hall. They hurried to their room and collided into each other as they both tried to enter at the same time while wearing their backpacks.

They shared a laugh and I giggled at how goofy they were together.

I took another drink of the cool sugar water that quenched my parched throat and watched Jill take a step back to let Jenny enter first. Once the last backpack disappeared into their room, I heard laughing, bags being unzipped, and what must've been whatever toys they brought back being dumped all over the floor.

The garage/utility room door opened again, and this time Dad stepped inside carrying a carton of Burger King drinks. He looked at me sipping my Mountain Dew.

"I guess we'll save your Coke until later."

Normally, I would've put up a fight and just chugged the green drink and then had the Coke with my meal, but that was the furthest thing from my mind. I watched as Dad held the door for Mom as she carried her purse, two large brown paper bags with the Burger King logo on them, and two cardboard kids' meals. No matter how hard I tried, I couldn't find an entry point into this conversation that I knew had to happen.

"Do you mind, son?"

I didn't even realize that I was standing in the middle of the kitchen.

"Sorry," I said, backing up from the door and sitting on the kitchen counter.

"No problem."

The two of them walked inside and set all the food and drinks down on the table. My dad's eyes looked heavy, and his hair wasn't combed like it normally was. Mom had her hair in a bun and sported dark circles under her eyes. It appeared as though I was the only one in the house who got any sleep.

"Mav, how are you doing?" Mom asked, approaching me.

She placed her hands on the knees of my swinging legs that I was unaware were moving. "Are you okay?"

"Umm," I thought hard about what to say next. Too hard apparently, because, in my silence, Dad turned around and waited for me to speak. "I have something else I need to tell you."

The two of them were fully alert now, and their eyes revealed more concern than I think they intended.

"It's about the walkie-talkies," I said.

"What about them?" Dad said.

Mom's stare intensified.

"Uhh, when I went to my room last night, I took the walkie-talkie with me. I got in bed and turned it on, but it was only static at first. I told you how I heard Max near the train tracks, you know?"

They both nodded.

"Well," I said and looked at the floor. "I heard him again."

"You what?" Mom said, closing the gap between us and stepping in front of my dad like she was boxing out for a rebound.

I met her gaze.

"When I went to my room, I pressed the button and called for him." Dad homed in on me, hanging on every word. "I must've said his name five or ten times . . . I don't know. But just when I was about to call it quits—well, I never really thought he'd answer in the first place—but when I was about to call it quits, he said my name."

They stared at me like they were waiting for me to continue.

"I made sure it was him, and it was."

"How do you know?" Mom asked.

"What do you mean?"

"I mean, how do you know it was Max? There are people

who listen to police radios, like weirdos who have no lives and get off on that kind of thing. Maybe one of them heard the call over the police radio and somehow stumbled upon the same frequency your walkie-talkie was on," she said, but even as she finished her thought, her own tone admitted that theory was a bit far-fetched.

Dad just looked at her like she was reaching—which she was—and then back to me.

"Tell us exactly what was said."

"Yeah, so Max said that he was still in the tunnel. He said he could see the sheriff and other cops looking for him and even saw their cop car lights. It was so weird."

"Did he say he was hiding in the tunnel?" Dad asked with a sudden alarm in his voice.

I hesitated, not really sure how to answer that because I wasn't sure if Max had even said that. I also knew I had to tell them the really weird part.

"He said he could see his dad and Blake's dad in there looking for him."

"So, he was hiding in the tunnel?" Dad practically screamed.

"He said he was in . . . 'the dark place.' He said he was with his mom."

Dad furrowed his brow. Mom eyeballed him and then me.

"I know how crazy it sounds, but the last thing he said was that he—whoever 'he' is—was going to let him go tonight. Max said he was going to come and visit me."

Dad rubbed his chin and took a step back, thinking for only one second and then turning around to grab the phone.

"Who are you calling, Roger?"

"Sheriff Potts. Either Max was hiding in the tunnel playing a joke, or he's hurt or, God forbid, someone . . ."

Sheriff Potts must've picked up on the other end because Dad abruptly switched gears.

"Yes, hello. This is Roger Hall. I'm trying to reach Sheriff Potts. Is he in?"

I heard a muffled voice on the other end.

"Uh-huh. Sure, I'll hold."

I glanced at Mom who only stared at Dad as she fidgeted with her fingernails. A louder muffled voice said something on the other end of the line.

"Hi, Sheriff. I think I have something you need to hear."

". . . . ."

"Well, I just got home, and Mav told me quite a tale."

". . . . ."

"He said he spoke with Max again on the walkie-talkie last night."

". . . . ."

"Yeah, and he said that Max saw you, Walt, and Joel in the tunnel. Even said he saw his mother."

". . . . ."

"Yes, she's been gone quite some time now."

". . . . ."

"Yes, he also said that Max said he would come and see him tonight . . . That whoever was with him was going to let him go."

". . . . ."

"You do? Do you really think that's a good idea?"

". . . . ."

"Okay then. One second."

Dad pulled the phone from the side of his face and covered the receiver with his other hand.

"He wants to talk to Mav," he told Mom, and then to me, "Can you tell the sheriff what you just told us?"

Mom bit her lip, still picking away at her polished nails.

"I can," I said. "I don't have anything else to tell him other than what you just said, though."

Dad extended the phone toward me.

"That's okay. I think he needs to hear it from you just the same."

I hopped off the counter and took the phone. The plastic receiver was warm on my ear.

"Hello?"

"Hi, Mav. It's Sheriff Potts. How are you doing today?"

"I'm okay."

"That's good to hear."

An uncomfortable silence hummed in our phone lines.

"Listen, Mav, do you care to tell me what happened with the walkie-talkies? Your dad just filled me in, but I want to jot down some notes from what you say."

"Okay," I said, then proceeded to recite the story for the second time that afternoon. After I told him everything that Dad just did, I added, "Do you think someone has him?"

"I don't know," Sheriff Potts said without hesitation.

I appreciated the way he talked to me. He didn't sugarcoat it or lie to make me feel better; he talked to me like I was an adult.

"What do you think?" he asked me.

I looked at Mom and Dad who were watching me like I was a wobbling Jenga tower.

"He said he was in the dark place with his mom. I think he's dead."

Mom gasped. Dad stepped forward and snatched the phone from my hands. He immediately put it to his ear and began speaking.

"Sheriff, I'm going to cut this off. We need to talk with Mav about this."

".........."

"Yes. Thank you for understanding. Please keep us updated after you check it out."

".........."

"Wait!" I blurted. "I have to tell him one more thing."

Dad's eyes looked like they were about to pop.

"What do you need to tell him?"

"Can I please just tell him?"

".........."

Whatever the sheriff said made my dad sigh and hand the phone back to me.

"Sheriff?"

"Yes, Mav?"

"When I say I think he's dead, I don't mean that I think a person killed him."

Mom and Dad exchanged worried glances again.

"Do you think he got hit by the red car?"

"I . . . I, uh, honestly don't know. I don't think so. I just got this feeling when I was talking to him that he wasn't here . . . like, in our world. I know that sounds weird."

"What made you think that?"

"He was calm. Like he had all the answers. Max is never like that."

"I see. But he did say that he'd come and see you tonight, right?"

"Yes."

"So just to recap this, Mav, you think Max is dead or gone or just not here with us anymore, but he's going to visit you tonight? And you think this because he told you through the walkie-talkie last night?"

"Yes."

"Mav, could this have all been just a dream?"

His question was a punch to the gut.

"What?"

"Think about it. Max was no doubt on your mind when you were going to bed. You're a smart kid. I'm just saying there's a chance that you were dreaming, you know?"

I felt my face flush, half from anger, half from embarrassment from the fact that he could've been right. For a split second, I entertained the latter. It was more comforting—more convenient—for me to believe that I called out for Max and fell asleep, allowing my subconscious to answer on his behalf. I wanted to accept it, but I knew it wasn't true.

"I wasn't dreaming," I said. "Or if I was, it felt too real for me to know the difference."

"That's all right. How we're going to proceed won't be affected either way. We've temporarily shut down the tunnel, and we're doing everything in our power to locate him. If what you said wasn't a dream, and what Max said is true and he does show up at your house tonight, that would be a good thing, right?"

I thought about the way Max had said he'd come and see me. It didn't sound like it would be a good thing.

"Yes," I lied.

"All right, then. Your parents will keep you safe either way, Mav. Now can I speak with your dad again?"

"Yes, sir."

I handed the phone back to Dad.

"Hi, Sheriff."

". . . . ."

"Yes, I see what you mean. I didn't sleep a wink last night, and when he told us that just now, I didn't think twice about it."

". . . . ."

"I agree. That's the more logical conclusion."

"........"

"You're welcome. Yes, I'll keep you updated."

"........"

"Okay. You too. Goodbye."

Dad hung up the phone and put his hands on his hips with his back to us.

"Dad, I wasn't dreaming."

Mom put her hand on my shoulder.

"It's okay, honey," she said. "We're going to figure all this out."

"Like they figured everything out with Max's mom?" I blurted out, not thinking before I said it.

Dad pounded his hand on the table, rattling the Burger King bags and drinks.

"Stop, Mav," he said and then took a deep breath, regaining his composure. "Just, please, stop."

I didn't know what to say or do. I just stood there like a Sears mannequin. Mom reached into one of the bags and searched around until she found what she was looking for. She handed me a burger, fries, and some napkins.

"Here," she said. "You need to eat."

I looked at my dad as he rubbed his eyes and returned my gaze.

"Sorry, buddy. I'm just . . . sorry."

"I'm going to go eat with Jenny and Jill," I said and walked out of the kitchen.

"Mav," Dad said.

I stopped but didn't turn around.

"Happy birthday."

I had completely forgotten.

The day passed like a blur. Nothing eventful happened. No new leads on Max that we were made aware of. I spent most of the time playing board games or toys with the twins. We watched The Mighty Ducks and ate a bag of Cheetos. The phone rang a few times. Each time it did, I poked my head into the hallway, hoping to hear that they found Max and he was okay, but of course that call never came.

The three of us were in the middle of a game of Guess Who? when I told them I had to go to the bathroom. I really did have to pee, but that's not why I went. The dread and sadness that had been snowballing in me all day demanded to come out. I just started crying as soon as I saw my reflection. It came uncontrollably, and I had to turn on the water faucet to mask my bawling. After a good three minutes, I washed and dried my face.

Mom called us for dinner just as I stepped into the hallway. We ate in relative silence. Normally, Dad would try to keep some sort of conversation afloat, but he just stared at his plate and took slow, robotic bites of chicken alfredo. Only Jenny and Jill made any noise other than chewing sounds. They both had a Barbie in one hand and a fork in the other as they made their dolls talk to each other while simultaneously nibbling away at chopped-up noodles.

I forced my food down. Normally, chicken alfredo was one of my favorite dinners, but I had no desire to eat. My stomach was in knots. I looked through the window over my dad's shoulder at the dimming world outside. The darker it got, the harder it became to think about anything other than Max.

"Roger," Mom said, breaking Dad from his trancelike state.

"Yes?"

"Do you want to make the kids some ice cream cones when you're finished?"

"Sure, I can do that. How about it? You guys want some ice cream when you're finished?" he asked with a forced smile.

"Yes!" the twins said at the same time.

He smiled more genuinely after their enthusiastic response and then looked at me. I didn't say anything.

"And you, birthday boy? Thirteen-year-olds get three scoops, right?"

I thought about eating pizza and cake with Max and Blake only twenty-four hours before and wanted to go back to that moment. I most definitely did not want three pity scoops of ice cream to try and distract me from the fact that my best friend was missing.

"Sure."

As promised, Dad served us dessert. The twins took their cones and asked me if I wanted to come back to their room. Apparently, they'd enjoyed hanging out with their big brother all day. I smiled but shook my head and told them I wanted some alone time. My rejection didn't faze them at all as they skipped down the hallway. I watched and waited for a dropped cone that never happened.

Dad handed me my triple-decker. I thanked him and crossed the kitchen to go to the utility room.

"Mav," he said.

I turned around.

"Are you okay?"

"Not really. I'm going to take a shower and watch a movie."

"I'd like to watch it with you. Anything you want."

Mom finished putting the dishes in the dishwasher and turned to us.

"I'll come if I'm invited," she said.

I didn't say anything.

"What?" she began. "Too cool to hang with your parents now that you're a teenager?"

"I just want to be alone right now."

Dad nodded his head.

"I understand, but after what you said about Max coming back tonight, I—"

"Dad, it was a dream."

He raised his eyebrows above his glasses.

"I've thought about it all day, and the sheriff is right. It was just a dream."

"I'd be lying if I said I wasn't happy to hear that," Mom said. "You had me worried." She hugged me. "They'll find him, honey. It'll be okay."

When she let go of me, Dad patted my back.

"I love you, buddy. I'm sorry this had to happen on your birthday. My hope is that we get a call from the sheriff saying they found him."

I fake smiled. "That'd be the best birthday present," I said and took a big bite of ice cream to really sell them on it.

"All right, buddy. Enjoy your movie," Dad said.

I walked out of the kitchen, through the utility room, and into my room, shutting the door behind me. The windows and sliding glass doors that lined every wall were all dark and had never been so intimidating. I dropped my ice cream cone in the trash and turned left to take a shower.

Steam filled the small bathroom as I sat in the tub letting the hot water spill down on me. My arms were wrapped around my bent legs like I was about to do a cannonball into a pool. I rested my forehead on my knees and wept. When the hot water started to turn lukewarm, I finally washed myself and got out. I grabbed my white fluffy towel and dried off.

My dresser stood against the wall to my right when I exited the bathroom with the towel wrapped around my waist. I put on some gym shorts and a T-shirt and headed for the corner of the room where the couch and TV setup waited. Event Horizon half-hung out of the mouth of the VCR. We'd let it play through to the point that it rewound itself and ejected. I took it out and put it back in its rightful spot in my collection and scanned the titles for something to watch.

For the first time that day, I had a genuine laugh when my eyes landed on the chosen film: The Lost Boys. Max loved it, but I always thought it was overhyped and still do. I grabbed it and put it in the VCR. The blue TV screen turned black as previews for old movies began to play. I picked up the remote and fast-forwarded to the opening scene.

And then I just sat there. I stared at the screen, but my mind was a dial tone. Thinking back on it now, I realize that I was still in a state of shock that hit intermittently since the incident. Halfway through the movie, Mom came to check on me. She asked if I wanted some popcorn or anything else, and I told her no. I reassured her that I really was okay. She handed me the pillow and blanket from my bed and practically pushed me over on the couch to tuck me in. She kissed my forehead and told me not to stay up too late. She finally left me alone, and at some point during the vampire home invasion in the climax of the movie, I fell asleep.

A tapping on the window stirred me. The TV had turned blue, and The Lost Boys now poked out of the VCR, waiting to be put back on the shelf. I squinted at the bright blue light and shielded it with my hand. The digital clock below read 1:11 a.m. I reached for the remote and hit the <**POWER**> button.

The room went dark, and I could finally see everything. An outline of someone's head stared at me through the window behind the TV. It took my mind a second to accept it, but once I did, an icy feeling shocked my system. The person raised their hand and tapped three times on the window. It wasn't a grown-up. I could tell that from the person's skinny arm and height.

"Mav," the shadow said.

I took shallow breaths. My heartbeat reverberated in my ears.

Is this a dream?

"Mav, it's me, Max."

I still couldn't bring myself to say anything, only stare at the person outside, separated from me by only a frail pane of glass.

"Mav, I can see you. Let me in, man. It's okay."

I looked through the adjacent windows at my parents' side of the house and saw their lights were off. When I looked back, Max was standing at the sliding glass door beside the TV. I bolted upright and flung the covers off me. From this angle, I could see more of him in the moonlight, and it was definitely Max. He was wearing the same clothes from the last time I saw him and held something in his hand. He must've noticed me trying to make out what it was because he lifted up the object and held it to the window: the other walkie-talkie.

"Max?"

"Yeah, dude. I told you they were going to let me go tonight. Why are you acting so weird? Let me in. I can tell you everything now."

I stood up on rubbery legs. Part of me wanted to scream for joy that my friend wasn't dead, but another part told me this was too good to be true. Max watched me as I made my way to the door. Looking at him up close made me feel so much better. It was him. He wasn't some rotting, decrepit corpse or floating, pale vampire; he was just my friend. I reached down and grabbed the wooden dowel that lay in the door's metal track which served as a door jam.

Max wasted no time opening the door. He walked inside, and a stench followed him. I watched him look around the dark room like he'd never seen it before. When I shut the door that he neglected to close, he turned around to face me.

"Where have you been?" I asked, still holding the three-foot piece of wood.

He smiled.

"I told you already. I went to the dark place. The same place my mom went. She got out like me once, but she's back there now. That's why my dad is so messed up. I know how to make him happy again. I want to get her out for good."

I leaned against the sliding glass door, trying to make sense of this. Max broke the silence with a wet cough like he'd just choked on spit. He coughed again and hacked up something into his hands, then wiped whatever it was on his pants.

"Are you okay?" I asked. "What you're saying isn't making sense, and you smell like freakin' roadkill."

"There's a place in that tunnel," he said, taking a step

toward me. "It's not always there, only when it wants to be, I guess. Redness, that's what it is. When I went through it, it felt like water, like I was being pulled to the bottom of a dark, cold pool, but I could breathe. I could see the hole in the tunnel, but it was so far away. And there was this thing in there with me. I could only see its shape when it moved. It was slithery like a snake but stood upright. I'm not sure, but I think it had tentacles. It never let me fully see it, but it talked to me. It told me the rules—"

"What rules?" I interrupted, completely wrapped up in his story.

"Time works differently there, too," he said, seemingly ignoring my inquiry. "I remember talking to you and Blake and then a second later, you were calling from your house. How is that possible?"

"I don't know, Max, but I think it's time we go wake up my parents."

"Why?" he asked, taking another step and coughing up more of that slimy stuff into his hand.

"What do you mean, 'Why?' You've been missing. You're here now. We need to let the police know and get you home or . . . see a doctor or something."

"No, Mav," he said in a raspier voice that sounded like he had a cold. "Those aren't the rules. That's not how this works. That's not what it wants, and it's not how I get my mom back."

"You sound nuts!"

"Come with me, Mav. Come back to the tunnel with me, and I'll show you I'm not crazy."

"Hell no. I'm getting Dad," I said and attempted to walk around him.

He grabbed my arm.

"Don't," he said.

69

I looked into his eyes and saw a faint blue light in the center of his pupils.

"Let go of me."

"Please, come with me. You have to come willingly. That's a rule."

I jerked my arm free.

"Seriously, stop it with these stupid rules. I'm getting my dad. You need help."

I stormed past him and stopped when I heard the growling behind me. When I turned around, Max's eyes were glowing blue. His lips curled back in a snarl, and black slime oozed out of his mouth and down his shirt. The room now reeked of rot. He sprinted toward me. I raised the wooden door jam and swung for his head, but he caught it with an impossible quickness and jerked it from my hand.

"Fine," a voice that sounded nothing like Max's said. "If you won't come willingly, I know at least two people in this house who love that tunnel."

I thought of Jenny and Jill who insisted on rolling down their windows every time we drove through the tunnel to smell the creosote-treated wood.

"No!"

He swung so fast that I didn't even see it. I heard a sickening crack, and the front of my face went numb. The dark room spun as I dropped to the floor. I fought to see, but my brain was shutting down. Warm liquid poured down my face, and just before I passed out, I heard him say, "Jenny or Jill? Who will it be?"

PART FIVE
ECHOES

When I think back on that night, on that specific moment of Max's return from the beyond, I can unreservedly say that I was never the same. I couldn't process it at the time, but my perception of life, death, the universe, and our place in it fundamentally changed. Everything I'd been taught in school or heard in church hadn't prepared me for this knowledge.

At the age of thirteen, I was cursed with a glimpse behind the cosmic curtain. Max returning from where he'd been and the existential ramifications that entailed have dwelled in me since that night, hibernating somewhere in my subconscious. I've managed to live with this knowledge for over twenty-four years now, but this last one has been the worst. Whatever self-preservation mode in which my mind reverted to carry me through life is running out of fuel. I feel my ability to differentiate what is real from what is not tearing apart at the seams.

The beast in me wants out. I feel it looking through my eyes at the world just like Max had said he'd viewed the world through that narrow slit when he fell into the tunnel. Honestly, it surprises me that I've lasted this long.

Put yourself in my position. How would you get up and go to school, to work, to the grocery store, pretending that there isn't a world beyond ours full of darkness that wants nothing more than to rip through the fabric of the physical universe and snatch us out of existence, one by one? Medication, therapy, booze, and lots and lots of suppression are the strategies I've employed to face each day since I was thirteen.

Now I just want to finish it.

The sound of my bedroom door swinging open and banging against my dresser broke me from my slumber, but the immediate brightness of the light being turned on is what really woke me up.

"Where is she? Where is she?" I heard my mom frantically saying. "Is she out here, Maverick?"

I squinted to open my eyes. I looked out the windows and saw that it was still dark outside. The clock under the TV displayed 3:13 a.m. When I propped myself on my elbow, I realized that I still lay on the floor. It took me a moment to remember how I'd ended up there.

Max.

"Oh my God!" Mom said as she rushed over to me.

I blinked and looked at her. She squatted down beside me and placed her hands on the sides of my face, examining me like a doctor. As soon as she applied the slightest pressure, electric shocks of pain shot through my skull. I winced and recoiled.

"What happened to you?"

It was then that I noticed the blood on the carpet where my head had been. I touched my forehead and worked my fingertips down. The structure of my nose had been altered. Where once it had protruded straight out, now it dented at the bridge and curved to the left.

"Ow, shit!" I said, not really caring about cursing in front of my mom at this point.

The memory of Max with the wooden dowel and the way he decked me with the strength of a major league baseball player replayed in my mind.

"What happened to you?" she asked. "Where's Jenny?"

I sat all the way up and looked around the room. I saw the wooden door jam on the carpet by the couch. The end that had broken my nose was splintered and covered in blood. My eyes followed the carpet until they reached the sliding glass door. A sliver of moonlight shone through the crack in the opening from where it hadn't been shut all the way.

This was real.

"It was Max," I said. The more I thought about it, the more enraged I became. "It was Max. I told you all he was coming back for me, and you didn't believe me!" I stood up and looked at my mom who had a shocked look on her face.

"You said it was a dream—"

"He came in here and wanted to take me to the tunnel. I wouldn't go with him, so he whacked me with that thing and said he was going to take one of the twins."

Her eyes widened.

"Oh no," she said and grabbed my wrist. "Come on. We have to go."

We walked into a fully lit kitchen. The walkie-talkie was on the kitchen table. My mom dragged me past it and into the living room, which blinded me even more. The room was full of blurry people until I wiped my eyes.

Dad was holding Jill. She had her head resting on his shoulder and her legs dangling down around his waist. He looked even more tired than the last time I'd seen him. His hair was messy, and he slouched as he readjusted his grip on my sister. He stood beside Sheriff Potts who looked fully alert with his 7-Eleven cup of coffee. Joel sat on the couch, slumped over, and staring at the coffee table until he saw me. He stood up.

"Good God, what the hell happened to you?" he asked.

Dad finally looked my way and saw my busted face. I watched his weariness give way to panic as he switched his gaze from me to Mom and back to me again. He walked over to us.

"Mav, who did this?" Dad asked.

"It was Max," I said.

Dad's brow furrowed just enough to let me know he'd fucked up in believing that I'd dreamt it all along. Two hands gripped my shoulders and yanked me, and I was suddenly face-to-face with Joel, who didn't reek of booze, surprisingly.

"What do you mean it was Max? He was here?" he asked, his eyes held the sobering intensity of a courtroom trial lawyer.

Sheriff Potts put his hand on Joel's shoulder.

"I'll take it from here, Mr. McNeil," he said, not removing his hand from Joel's shoulder until Joel removed his from mine.

Joel let go and took a step back. The sheriff addressed my mom behind me.

"It's best to keep everyone here, so let's avoid taking him to the hospital tonight."

"Look at his nose. He needs to go to the emergency room," Mom said.

"It's just a broken nose," the sheriff said.

"'Just a broken nose,'" she echoed in disbelief.

"It just needs reset and bandaged," he said. "I used to box. I've seen much worse."

Mom still wasn't buying it.

"Look, my brother-in-law is a doctor. I can have him come out if it'll make you feel better," he said. "I'll call him in just a minute."

My dad nodded to her as he slowly rocked Jill who was still sleeping. Mom huffed but walked into the kitchen and called 9-1-1. I listened to her end of the brief call.

"Who did that to your nose, son?" Sheriff Potts asked.

"I told you. It was Max."

"Yes, you did. What happened after that?"

"I fell down, and he said he was going to get one of the twins to take to the tunnel."

"The tunnel?"

"Yes." I looked around, knowing Jenny wasn't here but hoping that she might be hiding behind the couch or behind a curtain, anything but this. I swallowed hard and asked, "He really did take her, didn't he?"

"Well, she's not here."

"We have to go to the tunnel," Dad said quickly, carefully placing Jill on the couch. "What are we still doing here?"

The sheriff turned around and walked past my dad to the door.

"I'm calling it in on the radio. I'll have deputies there as soon as possible."

"I'm going," Dad said. "Honey, stay with Max and Jill. Wait on the doctor."

In the midst of all the chaos, Joel looked like he had something else on his mind. I kept catching him staring at me.

"I'm coming," Mom said.

"We'll have enough people looking. It's best you stay with your other two kids," Sheriff Potts advised. "I'll get my brother-in-law out here." He looked at Joel. "What about you?"

Joel returned his gaze. "I'll wait here with them if it's okay with her. Might drive around the neighborhood. I don't know."

The sheriff shot him a look like he was from another planet and then turned toward the door.

"Find our baby, Roger," Mom said through gritted teeth. She was never the one to sit back and take orders, and I could tell she didn't like the duty she'd been assigned.

Dad nodded and left with the sheriff behind him. That left me, Mom, Joel, and Jill who was now snoring into a couch cushion.

True to his word, the sheriff's brother-in-law, a short man who called himself Dr. Bob, showed up and reset my nose as I sat in one of the chairs by the dormant fireplace. All I felt was pressure, then I heard a crack. It made me feel like Rocky Balboa in the ring, and for just a second, I felt like a tough guy. He bandaged me up and left just as quickly as he'd come.

As soon as the front door shut, Joel, who'd been sitting in the matching chair on the other side of the fireplace, stood. Mom was lying on the couch beside Jill, stroking my sleeping sister's hair and glaring out the window.

"Mav, do you mind showing me your room where all this happened?" he asked, then looked at my mom. "That all right?"

She didn't break her gaze from the front yard.

"Sure."

"Can we do that?" he asked me.

"Yeah, okay," I said, not really knowing what he was planning to find out by looking at my room. Joel was no Sherlock

Holmes. If anything, that would've been Blake's dad, I remember thinking.

I led Joel to my wing of the house. The overhead light was still on. The spot of blood on the carpet looked darker and harder.

"That's where he hit me."

Joel approached the wooden door jam and examined the bludgeoning tool.

"What's this black stuff on the stick?"

"Probably blood," I said.

He picked up the dowel with his thumb and index finger as if he didn't want to contaminate it with fingerprints. He brought it closer to my face.

"Nope. This is blood," he said, pointing to the splintered end. "This is not blood. What is it and where did it come from?"

A memory of Max's distorted face, oozing what looked like tar from his mouth flashed through my mind.

"I don't know, but it came from Max."

Joel didn't look shocked.

"I'm surprised it's still here," he said.

"What do you mean?"

"Nothing."

He turned and faced the sliding glass door where Max had entered and walked over to it, examining it before pulling it open. He inspected the wooden deck that led to the pool.

"What is it?" I asked.

"There are muddy footprints out here."

I approached him and looked outside. A set of shoeprints dotted the deck coming in from the grass and a slightly less dirty track led back into the yard. I looked at the carpet and noticed the dry smudges of mud leading up to where Max had hit me in the face.

Joel stepped outside and trudged across the backyard without saying anything. I instinctively followed as he walked what I presumed was Max's path. The squishy grass was still damp from a brief summer shower earlier that evening. Joel didn't bother to look to his right at the U-shaped house. He kept moving until he reached the chain-link fence that connected to the end of Mom and Dad's side of the house.

The fence was wide open.

"You normally leave your gate like this?"

"No. Never."

Joel stepped through it and turned right, walking parallel with the house. He studied the side of it as he moved.

"Which one of these is your sisters' roo—"

He stopped before I could respond.

"Oh man," I said, staring at a partially open window.

Joel looked at the grass that led to the road, and the road that led to the tracks. He put his hands on his hips and sighed.

"Not again," he said to himself.

"What do you mean?"

He turned around.

"Nothing. Just pray the cops made it there before that thing and your sister did."

I was so caught off guard that he would refer to his son as "that thing" that I didn't realize he'd already made it to the front yard. I hurried to him as he neared his truck.

"Where are you going?"

"Home."

I ran as fast as I could and grabbed the passenger side door handle just as he started the engine, pulling the door open before he could take off. He glared at me, and I saw the tears in his eyes.

"What's going on?" I asked.

"Shut the door, son. You need to be inside with your mom and sister. Don't need to be out here in the night."

"Why? Please talk to me. Max is my best friend and now he has Jenny. You have to tell me what's going on," I insisted, suppressing the urge to completely break down.

He grabbed the gearshift like he was going to take off with me standing there. Without thinking, I jumped in and shut the door behind me.

"What the hell do you think you're doing?"

"I'm not going anywhere until you tell me what's going on," I said, shocking myself for talking to Joel like that.

He stared into my eyes with gritted teeth. I refused to break contact or even blink.

"Okay," he said, then looked past me at the front of my house.

I followed his gaze and saw Mom approaching with the front door still open.

"Roll down your window," he said.

Mom trudged across the grass.

"What the hell do you think you're doing?"

"That's a good question," Joel said, peering at me.

"I'm going with Joel to the other end of the neighborhood."

"What? No, you're not. Get back inside right now, Maverick. Your sister is missing."

"Yeah, I know. Sitting in there isn't going to help anything."

"Absolutely not. Get—"

"All right, I asked him to do a favor for me," Joel interrupted. "It's something I can't do myself, and I promise we'll be back in twenty minutes."

I tried to not act surprised, because I had no idea what he was talking about or why he'd lied for me.

Mom just scowled at him like she was waiting for further explanation.

"I need him to pour my booze out," Joel said while staring at the road.

I just nodded my head.

"What?"

"I can't be of any use to anyone if I'm half-sauced. It very well could be too late for my boy, but I might be able to save your daughter."

"You don't need my son—"

"Leah, please. Twenty minutes."

I turned from Joel to Mom.

"I'll be right back," I said.

"Joel, if you're not back here in twenty minutes, I swear to Holy Christ . . ."

"Twenty minutes."

The truck lunged forward as Joel shifted into first gear and accelerated.

"Do you really need me to do that?" I asked.

"No."

"Why'd you call Max a 'thing'?" I asked as he shifted into second gear and then third.

"Max is dead, Mav."

My heart sank to my stomach.

"What?"

"My boy died the second he disappeared in that tunnel."

"He was in my room—"

"That wasn't him. That was its version of him."

"How do you know that?"

"Because it's happened before! Goddamn, you ask a lot of questions."

I looked out the window at the houses passing by and realized we were halfway to Joel and Max's house.

"What do you mean?"

Joel wiped tears from his eyes and sniffed.

"What I'm about to tell you . . . only one other person knows about, and I'm only telling you because it might save your life."

I stared and waited for him to work up the nerve to tell me whatever it was he had to say, but he just reached into the truck's cupholder and grabbed his pack of cigarettes, pulled one out, and lit it just before pulling into his driveway. He turned off the engine and cracked his window; I rolled mine down all the way.

"Not long after Max was born, Darla disappeared—Max's mom," he said, like I didn't already know that. "Everyone thinks she left us—well, me—thinks she just up and disappeared. And I let them think it. It's better that way. It's better they think I'm crazy.

"Truth is, she was going to 7-Eleven to get some smokes and milk because I forgot to pick them up on the way home. It had been raining, and she could've hydroplaned just before going inside. She must've lost control of the car in the tunnel. Only thing is that she didn't hit anything. She should've crashed straight into the slats, but she kept going forward, into darkness because they never found a car, let alone a crash."

"What color car was it?" I asked.

Joel diverted his blank stare from the windshield to me.

"What color was her car?" I repeated.

"Red. It was a red Thunderbird. She loved that car."

"Blake said it was a red car that almost hit us. Max was riding a red bike."

"Salt in the fuckin' wounds," he said and shook his head, seemingly unsurprised.

"Joel, how do you know all this? About your wife, I mean. If you weren't with her, then how—"

"Oh, she came back later that night."

A cold chill ran through me.

"She'd been gone an hour. Max was asleep. I was getting pissed thinking she'd decided to run into town for food or something. She was always flaky like that, though. That's why no one doubted it when she disappeared. I always had a suspicion that she had some other guy on the side, but I could never catch her in it. When I did, I thought I'd be prepared for it. Boy, was I wrong!"

Joel looked away like he was embarrassed and continued to puff his cigarette.

"That doesn't matter now, though. Nothing does."

"What happened when she came back?"

"There was a knock at the door," he said. "A knock at midnight is never a good thing. When I looked through the peephole, I saw it was her standing there on the porch. I thought I'd locked the door without thinking, but I opened it. It wasn't locked. She just stood there on the porch looking at me. I asked her what she was doing, but she didn't say anything. It was like she was messed up on something.

"I went to turn the porch light on, and she walked inside before I could even flip the switch. She smelled something awful, like rot or roadkill. She didn't even look at me . . . just walked right in and found a seat in the living room. I thought she was in shock or something, so I ran over to her and kept asking her what was wrong. She didn't say anything. It was like she was in some kind of trance. I said her name and shook her, but it wasn't until I tapped on her cheek that she snapped out of it.

"I'll never forget the look in her eyes. It was my wife's body, but something else was staring out through those eyes. 'Joel?' she said, like she was just realizing who I was. I hugged her and told her it was me and asked her what happened. And that's when everything changed."

Joel paused, closed his eyes, and shook his head. He finished his cigarette and snubbed it out in the car ashtray.

"What was wrong with her?"

"She smiled the widest smile I'd ever seen on a human. Her eyes watered with joy, and she started laughing—giggling—like a six-year-old girl on Christmas morning. I thought she was delirious, so I got down on my knees, shook her again, and demanded that she tell me what happened to her. Her jaw dropped like a damn drawbridge and this black shit just spilled out. It wasn't like projectile vomiting or anything. It just flowed out like a water faucet.

It covered her body and the floor, and then it stopped. I went to pick her up to carry her to the car and that's when she started squealing and scratching like a cat. She bit my ear and damn near tore it off. You can still see the scar right here. She just kept saying, 'No, I have to show you something, Joel. I have to show you something.' I told her she needed to go to the doctor, but she wasn't hearing it. I knew this wasn't going anywhere, and I was worried that a piece of my ear was missing, so I entertained her.

"I finally said, 'Okay, what do you have to show me?' Well, she lit up like a pinball machine when I said that. She walked over to me and took me by the hands like she used to, but her hands were cold and limp now. She told me exactly what I just told you about losing control of her car and driving into what should've been the side of the tunnel but going straight through into the dark place.

"It all made sense to me then. She'd been in a car wreck and must've banged her head. I immediately opened the door and scanned the driveway. 'Where's your car, Darla?' I asked. She said, 'The tunnel has it now, but we don't need it. We can take yours. Take me back, Joel. Let's go together. You'll love it. And it'll love you.'

"That last line made the hairs on my arms stand on end. I walked back inside and shut the door behind me. 'What are you doing?' she asked. Her voice was panicky now. I told her I was calling nine-one-one if she wouldn't go to the hospital with me. I walked into the kitchen to grab the phone and that's when she did this."

Joel bowed his head so I could see the scar at the top of his skull.

"How'd she do that?"

"With a letter opener she grabbed off the secretary desk . . . Dug it in my scalp and sliced about two inches back until she reached my bald spot. I flung her off me, and she hit the ground hard. Turned around and she was lying on the ground sobbing —begging—me to come to the tunnel with her.

"I said, 'Enough with the fucking tunnel!' I think that's when she finally got the picture that I wasn't going anywhere with her. I remember seeing a complete change in her face like a demon just took over. She said, 'Fine, I'll take Max with me if you're not willing to come.'"

My heart skipped a beat.

"Wait," I began, "she said, 'willing to come'?"

"Yeah. Why?"

"That's exactly what Max said to me. He said I had to willingly go with him to the tunnel because those were 'the rules.'"

"Well, Darla never said anything about rules, but she made for the stairs after Max. I caught her halfway up, wrapped my arms around her from behind, and just bear-hugged her. She fought me the whole way down and when I drug her across the living room and into the basement, I damn near tripped carrying her down those flimsy-ass steps, but I got her down there.

"As soon as I dropped her, she crawled over to the corner and started sobbing. By this point, I didn't know which way was up—my head was leaking down the back of my neck, the tip of my ear was barely hanging on, and I could hear Max crying upstairs from all the way down in the basement.

"I told her that she was staying down there until the paramedics showed up. She finally seemed like she'd given up and didn't say anything. I headed back up the steps and just when I reached the top of the staircase, I heard her behind me. She must've lunged at me right when I turned around because my elbow collided with her temple. It spun her backward, and she landed headfirst on the steps and kept rolling until she smacked into the wall at the bottom."

Joel wiped more tears from his eyes, took out another cigarette, and lit it.

"Do you want one?" he asked, extending the open pack toward me. "They're gross, but they make you feel better."

"No, thanks," I said, not really sure if he was being serious or not. Looking back on it now, I realize that he'd confessed so much at that point that giving a kid a smoke was the least of his concerns. "What happened to her? To Darla?"

Joel leaned back in the seat and took a long draw.

"My wife died in that tunnel. Whatever's in there chewed her up and spit out some kind of imitation. That thing that showed up at our house that night didn't move after I knocked it down the stairs. I started walking back down to see if it was dead, and that's when its head spun around. Goddamn neck snapped like a tree branch and her eyes were fixed on me, only they weren't eyes anymore. It's hard to describe."

"I know what you mean," I said. "Max's eyes were . . . like that."

Joel closed his eyes and tears rolled down his cheeks.

"I should've left this place with him that night, but I thought it was over. I can't tell you how many times I've been to that tunnel and checked it end to end and never found anything. I don't know why the universe just decided to snatch everything I love out of this world, but here we are. First Darla, now Max. Someone's gotta put a stop to it."

"What happened to Darla?"

"I ran out of there like a damn coward. I didn't know what else to do. I didn't know who to call anymore. After what I did to her body, I was terrified they'd take me to jail and/or take Max from me."

"So what'd you do?"

Joel looked at me. After a moment of consideration, he said, "This is another one of those parts you can't talk about because it involves somebody else and could get bad real quick for everyone if you do."

"I won't say anything."

"Walt—"

"Blake's dad?" I interrupted.

"Yes, Special Agent Walt."

Joel must've noticed my jaw drop because he actually cracked a smile for a second.

"I knew it!" I said. "We knew Walt was a fed—me and Max. Does Blake know?"

"Hell if I know, kid. All I know is that he wasn't an FBI agent then. He was working as a city cop and was still my friend at the time. I didn't know who else to call that I could trust.

"I called and told him it was an emergency. He was knocking on my door damn near as soon as I hung the phone up. I filled him in on Darla's disappearance and the thing claiming to be Darla showing up that night. I remember the way he looked at me, at all the blood on me, and I saw the fear in his eyes. He asked me what I did, and I told him to go to the basement and see for himself.

"I opened the door for him, and Darla was standing at the bottom of the staircase. Her neck was still snapped. She had taken all her clothes off. Her body was bruised and bloodied from the fight and the fall.

"'Darla—' he started to say, but she cut him off.

"I remember it as plain as day because it was a dagger through the heart. Darla said, 'Oh, hello, Walt. How long has it been since you've seen me naked? Do you still like what you see or is the blood too much for you? If I recall correctly, a little blood never stopped you before.'"

I had never been so uncomfortable in all my life. I didn't want to hear about my friends' parents being naked and killing each other. It was still too weird for me to watch movies with nudity in them with my mom and dad, and now I had to listen to this freaky stuff. But after my initial revulsion, I realized what Joel had just said. Walt, Blake's dad, had been screwing Darla, Joel's wife. Everything finally clicked as to why they always acted weird when they were forced to be near one another.

Joel looked at me like he was making sure I got the full picture. And judging by the way I just stared at the dashboard, slightly frowning, I think he registered what I felt.

"So the truth was out in the open for the first time. That naked thing pretending to be my wife had just outed Walt and Darla's affair. My suspicions of her infidelity had been

87

confirmed, but I never would've guessed it was Walt giving it to her."

"What did you say to him?" I forced myself to ask, still not looking away from the dashboard.

"I looked him in the eye and saw that in his shocked state, he had no strength to deny it. And he didn't. All he said was, 'I'm sorry, Joel.' Right at that point, Darla dropped down to all fours and climbed the staircase, bones snapping and joints popping.

"She lunged at us with her arms extended and teeth bared. The color in her eyes changed again, and she leaped up the last few stairs and just drilled me, completely knocking me on my ass. She started choking me, and I couldn't get her off. She was so much stronger than before. I thought my damn trachea was going to break. Next I heard Walt instructing and then demanding that she get off. I almost lost consciousness right before I heard a muffled boom!

"Her body just fell on top of mine. She wasn't breathing. I didn't even move until I felt a wetness on my face. Walt rolled her off me, and I expected to see blood everywhere, but it was that same black shit she puked all over the house earlier. Nothing about that thing was Darla. I looked at Walt, who was just standing there speechless, holding his pistol in one hand and a throw pillow he'd used to silence the gunshot in the other."

Joel took a break to take a few puffs.

"I don't get it," I finally said.

"What's that?"

"Why don't the police know what happened to her? Didn't Walt tell them?"

Joel fixed his gaze on me with the intensity that had intimidated me my whole life and said, "We covered it up. I didn't leave Walt with much of a choice—not that he needed much convincing. The fact that he tried to silence his gunshot let me know that he didn't know if he was doing the right thing when he fired."

"What did you say to him?"

"I told him that unless he wanted me to ruin his marriage, he was going to help me get rid of that body and never talk about it again."

It took a minute for the gravity of what he'd just said to sink in. Before I could ask my next question, Joel answered it for me.

"We didn't have to do it, though—get rid of the body. We were getting cleaning supplies ready when she just . . . evaporated."

"Huh?"

"One minute her body was there, and the next it was disintegrating, floating up into the air like black ash and disappearing. Every black stain of ooze, every part of her just rose up and vanished like the tunnel was calling it back. Max was upstairs wailing his head off. I made him a bottle and sat in his bedroom and fed him while Walt and I figured out a way to cover up what really happened."

"How'd you do it?"

"Don't you remember what Walt told the sheriff last night?"

I thought back to Walt taking Sheriff Potts to the side and explaining that Joel thought the tunnel took Darla, but she really just left him and suffered from postpartum depression. Walt had said he knew this because Darla was close to his wife and had confided in her.

"You let people believe that your wife left you, and you sold it by acting like you were in denial, blaming the tunnel instead of yourself."

"Yep. Not the best plan, but it worked, especially with Walt vouching for it. With Walt involved, it was never even ruled a missing persons case. He went so far as to have a fake source claim they'd seen her in San Francisco. She didn't have any family except us, so people were more than happy to accept that story.

"Walt and I never talked about it again. I did my best raising Max, trying to act like everything was normal. It got easier as he got older and time passed. Sure, I drink when I think about it too much, and yeah, I've been hard on him at times, but I did my best. And this is where 'my best' got us—him dead the same way his mama died. And now your sister."

"You don't know that about Jenny," I said, but not really believing it. "For all you know, Dad and Sheriff Potts could have her right now, and what are we doing? Just sitting in your stupid truck in your stupid driveway."

Joel punched the steering wheel so hard that it honked the car horn. I jumped.

"You got in the truck with me, not the other way around. I came here to do one thing and one thing only, and I ended up telling a dumb kid way more than I should've, but I don't care anymore."

"What did you come here to do?"

"Something I should've done twelve years ago, but I couldn't leave Max. I got no excuse not to now."

Joel opened the truck door and stepped out.

"I'll be right back. I'm going to grab something and take you home."

I sat there and tried to process everything I'd just heard. My entire perception had been altered by one conversation. Everything I thought I knew had been a lie, and the adults were responsible for it.

The eerie absence of crickets chirping in the surrounding

darkness suddenly gave me the creeps. I reached over and rolled up Joel's window and locked the door. Something didn't feel right.

A few minutes later, Joel emerged carrying two black duffel bags, one draped over each shoulder. He walked past his door and carefully placed the bags in the bed of the truck, securing them with bungee cords. Before I could ask him what he was doing, he walked back into the house and emerged carrying a shotgun. He placed it behind our seats, and I didn't say a thing about it.

We stopped in front of my house a few minutes later. The sheriff's cruiser wasn't there, but Dad's car was still parked where he'd left it earlier. Joel didn't even bother pulling in the driveway. He kept both hands on the wheel and stared out the windshield. Before I got out, I asked, "What are you going to do?"

"Shut the door, Mav," he said without facing me. "You're a good kid. Stay that way."

I shut the door, and he drove off into the night toward the tracks that led to the road that dead-ended into the tunnel.

Mom opened the door with her arms folded.

Part of me screamed to do it, but the part that won out decided that Joel probably knew more about what to do than anyone else, and a morbid curiosity wanted to see if I was right.

Mom glared at me and let me lead the way inside.

"It's about time," she said. "Your father is still not back."

As if on cue, a set of headlights pulled into the driveway and shone in through the large living room window. We both peered through the pane into the darkness.

"It's the sheriff," Mom said.

Two doors opened, and two men got out. There was no sign of Jenny.

"They don't have her," Mom said, like she was about to lose it. "Oh Jesus, they don't have her."

She raced to the door to meet them. I stayed on the couch beside Jill who was still sleeping. I heard the door open and my mom ask, "Where is she? Where is she, Roger?" followed by sobbing. Her sobbing got louder as Dad escorted her into the house with the sheriff close behind.

"You didn't find her, did you?" I asked.

Dad, who was cradling Mom, looked at me and shook his head, and then I saw his face go pale as he stopped and stared at something behind me. Mom looked up at Dad, then followed his gaze and let out a bloodcurdling scream that made me jump. Even the sheriff took a step backward at what he saw. I slowly turned around to where Jill had been sleeping, but she was no longer on the couch.

She sat on the floor, her legs crossed and her back as rigid as a board. Her eyes had rolled back to the whites, and her mouth hung open. Without moving her lips or throat, a voice came from inside of her.

"Mommy? Daddy? It's Jenny. Where are you? I'm scared."

My skin crawled at the unnatural sight. Jill was being used like a walkie-talkie. And then it hit me. If Jenny was using Jill to communicate via some supernatural twin tethering, then that could mean only one thing: Jenny was in the tunnel.

PART SIX
THE TRAP

The night Jenny disappeared into the tunnel with what I'll, for simplicity's sake, refer to as Max, was the last time I saw my sister alive. After the events of the summer of 1999, Jill went on to live what would be considered a relatively normal life. She got married to her college sweetheart right after graduation and even had her own set of twins a couple of years later. She moved down south last year when her husband got a job offer too good to pass up.

Mom and Dad separated before my fourteenth birthday and were officially divorced shortly thereafter. After Jenny was taken, they became shells of their former selves. From what I remember, Dad started drinking too much and would come home complaining about work every day. He'd loved his job before the summer of 1999. He used to be a great guidance counselor, but when you hate yourself, it's kind of hard to care about others.

I sometimes put myself in his shoes. I can imagine seeing

every new girl walk into his office being a constant reminder of the daughter he'd lost. Maybe they had eyes like her, or said something the way she did, or looked like a slightly grown-up version of her, and then bitterness would set in when he realized Jenny would never get to experience that age or anything after. He'd never see her live her life and do all the things dads do with, and for, their daughters.

I'm guessing that's why he killed himself the following Christmas. When faced with such a loss, people can either cope with it and focus on the ones they have left, or they can choose to end their suffering when the pain becomes too great. At least he did it when Jill and I weren't at his new apartment. He left a note, but all he wrote was I'm sorry. There was no dedication. Mom assumed he was talking to us, but I feel like it was meant for Jenny. He never could forgive himself.

We moved to Harrisburg, about two hours away from Benson Valley. My mom wanted a fresh start for us, and despite Jill and I throwing hissy fits about missing our old friends, I think we both wanted to get the hell out of there too. It took a year or two, but we planted roots and settled in. We made new friends. Mom went on dates, which was weird at first but as I got older, I just wanted her to be happy. By the time I left for college, she had met and married my stepdad, Randy. He's a good guy. They live in South Carolina now, but I don't speak to them much.

Once I graduated college with a degree in philosophy and no job in sight, the only universal truth I knew was that I didn't know shit. I took a job investigating claims for an insurance company, basically either exposing fraud or screwing people over by finding loopholes that would permit my company to pay out as little as possible. The better at my job I became, the more I hated myself.

I work from home now as a regional supervisor. I make more money than I know what to do with. Occasionally, I have to travel and attend conferences, but ever since the pandemic, I never stopped working remotely. The solitude provided a false sense of comfort, and once I was fully withdrawn from society, slowly but surely, memories of Benson Valley began to inhabit my dreams.

Those nightmares started about two years ago, and the pain that I'd imagined my dad feeling leading up to his suicide began to grow in me. I was terrified to revisit the past, as I've stated before and will probably mention a few more times before I've said everything I know to say. I might've been done with Benson Valley, but Benson Valley was far from finished with me.

My dreams became more vivid. I'd wake up in the middle of the night convinced Max was floating outside my window, watching me. It got to the point where I'd be on a conference call for work and hear that static from the walkie-talkie and Max's voice would say, "Mav?" One time, I threw my headset off and ran from my computer during a Zoom meeting with my bosses.

I was in the shower not too long ago, and I couldn't take my eyes off the drain at my feet; the water being sucked down transfixed me. I stared into that darkness and heard Jenny's disembodied voice calling out to me, pleading for me to help her get out of the tunnel, the same way she did the night she disappeared.

About six months ago, I made up my mind to move back to Hillsbury County. I got online and looked for apartments downtown, but consciously or subconsciously—I'm not sure which—my search broadened to the outskirts of the city and into the suburban areas. A bunch of new subdivisions had popped up since I'd last seen the area nearly twenty years ago, but one kept calling to me: Golden Circle.

My filter for apartments had mysteriously vanished, and I fixated on this one house in Golden Circle that I hadn't seen since I lived in Benson Valley. The house on my laptop screen was a house I'd been in before. It no longer looked nearly as big as I'd remembered it. Not much had been changed from what I could tell, but it had been a relatively new construction back when we'd have sleepovers there. There were even two rocking chairs on the porch where Walt and Brandy had kept theirs many years ago.

The address on the listing—37 Benson Boulevard—gave me a shudder. I grew up on Benson Drive, and I'd always wanted to live on a "Boulevard." That was Blake's address, and this was his childhood home, which was, indeed, inside Benson Valley. I guess after the tragedy of the summer of 1999, the Benson Valley Homeowner's Association had deemed it necessary to change the name of the neighborhood. Rightfully so, I suppose. No one in his or her right mind would want to live in a subdivision notoriously known for disappearances and supernatural mysteries. I, however, was, and am, far from being in my right mind.

As if on autopilot, I contacted the real estate agent and put in an offer above the asking price even though the house had been on the market for more than three months. I had to have it. Benson Valley wanted me back. No, the tunnel wanted me back. I bought the house sight unseen, and within two weeks, I was driving a U-Haul back home, back to the one spot in the universe where I knew absolute evil existed. In fact, I was counting on it.

My dad stared at Jill who was still in that terrifying position, sitting on the floor cross-legged and mouth wide open. She didn't move. I don't think she took a breath, but memory could be playing tricks on me. Her appearance was even less human than a mannequin. It was like she was a character in a movie who'd been paused mid-scream.

"Jill?" Dad said as he neared her, but she didn't respond.

Mom and Sheriff Potts remained behind me. Dad inched his way closer and sat on the coffee table in front of her. He waved his hand in front of her frozen face. The shadow of his hand swiped back and forth across her eyes. Her pupils didn't even contract from the light.

"Mommy? Daddy?" Jenny's voice said from inside Jill. "Are you there?"

Mom brushed by me and ran to Jill's side.

"I'm here, baby. Where are you?"

"I'm in a dark place, Mommy. I'm scared. I want to come home."

"Who took you there?" Dad asked.

I looked back at Sheriff Potts, who didn't acknowledge me. He only watched the freak show happening in our living room. The man's mouth was open like he wanted to say something but couldn't process his thoughts enough to voice them.

"Max took me," Jenny's voice said.

Dad looked back at the sheriff. "What do you make of this?"

Sheriff Potts finally snapped out of his stupor and summoned his professional demeanor.

"I, uh, I don't know how your daughter's doing that, but you're not talking to Jenny," he said.

I looked sideways at him. "Yes, they are."

He glared at me. "It's impossible."

"No, it's not. They're twins. They have this connection."

"I've known twins," he began. "That doesn't mean they can speak through the other one like a damn ventriloquist dummy."

"Who's there, Daddy?"

"Me and Mommy and Mav. There's also a policeman here. We're trying to find you," Dad said.

"Where's Jill?"

We all exchanged baffled glances.

"Honey," Mom began, "you're talking through Jill."

"What do you mean?"

"Your voice is coming through your sister's mouth."

"What's going on, Mommy?"

"I don't know, but we're going to find you. Are you near the tunnel or did Max take you somewhere else?"

"I . . ." she began and then dropped down to a whisper. "Mommy, the monster is coming. I'm so scared."

I watched in horror as tears dribbled down Jill's face when Jenny began to sob.

"It's here," she whispered. "Mommy! Daddy! It's looking at me! It sees me!" Jenny screamed, and then Jill's head fell forward like the connection had been severed.

Dad lifted her face up and two black eyes stared back at him. He released her and stumbled backward. Mom gasped and covered her mouth. Jill started shaking violently, convulsing like she was having a seizure, and then fell backward, spasming on the floor.

"She's having a seizure," Sheriff Potts said as he hurried by me and dropped to one knee beside my sister.

I inched closer and saw that her eyes were all white now, and her eyelids drooped halfway closed. Her jaw was locked, and she shook so violently that I thought she was being electrocuted. In that moment, she looked like Regan from The Exorcist—a movie that, at that age, was too scary for me to watch by myself.

"Give me room," Sheriff Potts said.

Mom and Dad backed up.

"It's okay, sweetheart," Sheriff Potts said. He placed his hand under her neck and slid his hand between her head and the floor. "She's breathing just fine. It's a seizure. We just have to wait it out. It's scarier than it looks."

Jill stopped and looked up at the sheriff who was still addressing Mom and Dad. Her mouth opened and an emotionless imitation of Jenny's voice said, "It's letting me go. There's nothing to worry about."

Sheriff Potts looked down at my sister staring back at him, and I saw the terror in his eyes. My thirteen-year-old mind still fed off the fear of adults and seeing this man of the law so shook up made my stomach twist into knots.

"I'm coming out of the tunnel now. Please come and get meeee . . ." Her voice dropped down to a growl to finish out the last word.

Sheriff Potts removed his hand from under her head and backed away like he'd just touched someone with leprosy.

I thought about Joel, his gun, and whatever was in those two duffel bags he tied down in the bed of his truck.

"We have to go to the tunnel right now!"

Everyone looked at me in surprise.

"Joel's on his way there, and he has a gun."

"Jesus Christ," Sheriff Potts said.

"Mom? Dad?" Jill said—the real Jill—as she sat up, rubbing her eyes like she'd just awoken from a deep sleep.

Mom rushed to hug her while whispering comforting and reassuring things.

Sheriff Potts glanced at my dad.

"We need to go."

Dad nodded and regarded my mom. "Are you going to be okay here with them?"

"Yes, just go."

"I want to go," I said.

At the same time, Dad said, "No," and Sheriff Potts said, "Absolutely not."

I knew they'd say this, so I had my overreaction ready to go.

"All I want to do is help!" I stormed toward my room as quickly as possible. Once I made it to the utility room, I ran to the sliding glass door that led to the front yard. I jerked it open and sprinted to the driveway faster than I'd ever run in my life. I didn't look back until I reached Sheriff Potts's police car. Through the living room window, I could see the three of them wrapping up their conversation. I opened the door to the back seat and slid in, shutting it behind me as quietly as I could. The interior dome light dimmed right when I heard the front door of my house close. I curled into a ball on the floorboard behind the driver's seat and prayed they wouldn't see me.

Sheriff Potts opened his door and got in, and a second later, my dad did the same. Neither of them bothered to look in my direction. The car started up, and I listened as the sheriff picked up the car radio and called for backup, saying that there could be a possible situation at the tunnel.

That's the understatement of the week, I remember thinking.

As the car pulled out of the driveway, we began to move faster. I bounced when we sped over the train tracks and accelerated once we hit the main road. I listened as the engine revved, and we sped down the straight stretch and around the curves.

"I'm going to need you to stay in the car until I've secured the scene. Hopefully, we're not there alone for too long."

"If I see Joel roaming around with a gun, I'll have no problem waiting in the car."

"And what if we see your daughter?"

"I'll stay in the car until you've secured the scene."

"Thank you."

Sheriff Potts didn't know my dad, so he couldn't detect the lie. I knew just from his tone that Dad had no intention of staying in the car if we got there and saw Jenny.

"What in the hell?" Sheriff Potts said as we stopped.

"What is he doing?" Dad asked.

It took every ounce of energy for me not to try and sneak a peek at what they were seeing. All I could view was the FALLING ROCK sign through the rear passenger side window. Headlights—more than just the sheriff's—were present at the tunnel's entrance.

"Stay here." Sherriff Potts opened his door and took a slow step out.

I could tell he was only halfway standing out of the car by the way the weight shifted in the vehicle.

"What are you doing, Joel?" he hollered.

Screw it.

I had to see what was going on. As quietly as I could, I turned to my side and pushed myself up on my elbow. It gave me enough of a boost to see over the corner of the driver's seat.

Joel's truck was parked sideways across the tunnel's

entrance. There was no getting in or out; he had it completely blocked. The extra set of headlights I saw was because the front of his truck pointed directly at the falling rock side of the road. Even with the lights angled beside the tunnel, it gave him more than enough light inside to do whatever it was he had planned.

"Doing something I should've done a long time ago, Sheriff. Best you just turn around and leave me be."

Joel didn't even look at the sheriff when he spoke. He was too busy strapping something to one of the slats with what looked like copper tape. The longer I looked, the more bundles I saw taped to other slats, most of them installed around the left side of the tunnel where Max had disappeared. They looked like a bunch of red sticks all bound together by the copper tape, and that's when I realized what Joel was planning on doing.

Dynamite.

"I'm afraid I can't do that, Joel," Sheriff Potts said.

I looked at the man's waist and saw that the latch on his holstered pistol had been unbuckled. As far as I could see, Joel was unarmed, but I knew that he had that shotgun hidden somewhere back there.

"No?" Joel said, still going about the business of taping another bundle to a slat. "Afraid there's not much you can do about it now, Sheriff."

Sheriff Potts fully stepped out of the car and shut the door behind him. I watched as he took his time approaching the tunnel's entrance. My heart was beating so loud that I thought my dad would hear it, like in that Edgar Allan Poe story we had to read in school. Even though the sheriff kept getting closer, he kept his hands down by his side and made no movement like he was going for his gun.

Joel finished the last bundle he'd been working on and turned to face the approaching man of the law. He walked forward and leaned on the truck, resting his arms on the top. Sheriff Potts stopped about ten feet from him. He appeared to be looking at Joel's handiwork inside the tunnel.

"Is that what I think it is?"

"This tunnel should've been demolished the night Darla disappeared. There's so much you don't know, Sheriff."

Suddenly, the faint sound of police sirens could be heard in the distance, coming from the other side of the tunnel.

The sheriff's call for backup.

I anxiously waited for the flashing blue and red lights to come speeding through the tunnel, but they never did. I could see the hints of their headlights like they had stopped at the other end and refused to enter. The sheriff's radio screeched and then a voice spoke, "Sheriff, come in?"

Dad, who had been fully transfixed on the inevitable confrontation in front of him, jolted at the startling noise. He looked down at the handheld radio with its curly wire attached to the car.

"Sheriff, you there? There's a federal agent here saying they've got everything under control. His credentials are valid. What's going on?"

A federal agent ... Walt?!

Dad must've been thinking the same thing because he looked down at the radio and then back up at the situation unfolding in front of him, obviously unsure of what to do. He settled on rolling the window down and calling out to the sheriff.

"Sheriff Potts!"

The sheriff didn't turn around, but Joel shielded his eyes and tried to spot the source of the voice.

"Roger, is that you?" Joel asked.

"I told you to stay in the car," Sheriff Potts said.

"It's your deputies," Dad began. "They're calling for you on the radio."

"That's because they're on the other side of the tunnel. Joel, you've got nowhere to go."

Joel smiled and shook his head.

"They aren't coming. I've got my own backup."

"Shit," Dad said, opening the car door and stepping out. "They said there's a federal agent on the other side telling them the situation is under control."

Sheriff Potts turned his head to face my dad and had a bewildered look on his face. That's when Joel made his move. His shotgun must've been on the ground at his feet because he bent down, snatched it up, and leaped over the hood of the truck. When the sheriff turned around, Joel was on his side of the truck with the business end of the shotgun three feet away from the lawman's tin star.

"Walk to the car, fast."

The sheriff put his hands up and walked backward.

"Faster!" Joel said and racked the shotgun.

Sheriff Potts hurried to the car. I slid back down because even though the sheriff's back was to me, Joel would be looking right at me if he glanced in my direction.

"Whoa, whoa, Joel. What are you doing?" Dad asked. "We're all on the same team here."

"Roger, shut your fucking mouth and get back in the car."

Dad didn't move. Joel looked at him and had a crazy look on his sweaty face.

"Now!"

Dad shuffled back into the car and shut the door.

"Open your door, Sheriff," Joel commanded. "Get on that radio and tell them the feds are on this side too. They think the missing people here match the pattern of a cross-country killer."

Sheriff Potts opened his door and partially sat down. He reached over and grabbed the radio.

"Potts here," he said. "Sorry, it's busy on my end, too, with this jurisdictional bullshit."

"So what's going on, Sheriff?"

"The FBI seems to think this is a missing persons case in connection with several across the country. If there's an MO, they're not sharing intel with me. I think our night is over. Just head on back to the station, and I'll meet you as soon as I'm able."

"Roger, 10-4, boss."

The radio went silent, and Sheriff Potts placed it back on its holder.

"Done," he said to Joel, who I assumed was still standing near the car with the shotgun, though I couldn't see.

"Now turn around and go back home. You'll know when I'm done here."

"I can't let you blow up this tunnel, Joel," Sheriff Potts said.

"With all due respect, Sheriff, you don't have a choice."

I'm not sure what came over me in that moment, but I realized that if we left and Joel blew up the tunnel, Jenny would be gone for good. Yes, according to Joel, she was a goner already if Max took her to the tunnel, but this would eliminate any chance of getting her back . . . of getting Max back.

I readied myself and was about to leap up and tell them not to go when I heard Max's voice.

"Dad?"

The hairs on the back of my neck stood on end.

"I'll be goddamned," the sheriff said.

"That's . . . Max," Dad said.

I still couldn't see what they were seeing, just that my dad was looking out the sheriff's window. Neither one of the men in the front seat moved.

"Max? Max, is that really you?" Joel asked.

There's no way.

I took my chances of getting caught and slowly peeked out the window. Max stood beside the back of Joel's truck. Mostly silhouetted in darkness, the only light that shone on him came from the red taillights. I squinted and tried to detect any telltale signs of it being evil Max, but it was too hard to see with only the dim red glow.

"Dad, it's me," Max said.

Just as the sheriff started to open his door, Joel whipped around with the shotgun.

"I'm not fucking around with you two. Get out of here!"

"Okay, okay." The sheriff closed the door but didn't put the car in reverse or show any sign that he was leaving.

Joel turned back around, facing his son.

"Dad," Max began, "I did it. I brought Mom back."

I could see Joel shaking.

Come on, man. You can't believe this crap. You know what's really going on.

It proved to me how much people will ignore logic when they want to believe something. I thought back to Joel's story of Darla disappearing into ash.

He has to know Darla's gone for good.

I raised my head up a little higher for a better view. Sheriff Potts and Dad didn't see me. They were apparently just as transfixed by the scene outside as I was to be bothered by me in the back seat.

"That's not possible, son. Your mama's gone."

"She was gone, but she just needed someone to take her place. That's the rule. Come back here, Dad. She's right here behind the truck. Come see for yourself." Max backed up to give some space.

Joel took a few steps and then stopped short of the truck.

"Son, who'd you take into the tunnel?"

"What's it matter?"

"Did you trick Mav's little sister into going in there with you? Was that the trade?"

"So what if I did? Mom's back! Come see."

Joel clung to his gun and continued forward until he reached the back of the truck. From where I sat in the sheriff's car, I couldn't see what Joel was looking at. I only saw him from behind as he stared at something on the ground. I listened through the sheriff's rolled-down window.

"You see?" Max said. "I told you. It's her. We can be together again. You can be happy. We just need to get her back to the house so she can fully heal and—"

"Be quiet, Max," Joel said and kneeled out of sight, leaving only his right leg sticking out from behind the truck tire.

Sheriff Potts picked up the radio and clicked the button.

"One-nine, come in."

After a few seconds, a voice said, "One-nine here, Sheriff."

"We've got a situation here at the tunnel."

"Thought the feds were handling it, boss."

"There aren't any feds here. I don't know what's going on, but I was held at gunpoint and forced to say that. Send everyone we got out here now and tell them not to let anyone on that side of the tunnel stop them from getting through."

"On it, 10-4, Sheriff."

Sheriff Potts put the radio back down.

"I'm going over there," he said without taking his eyes off

the scene by the truck. "Don't get out of the car. If something happens to me, take the wheel and get the hell out of here."

Dad just nodded his head. He looked like he was in shock.

The sheriff opened the door without making a sound and slid out. He withdrew his pistol and crouched down as he made his way across the road.

"That isn't your mom, Max," Joel said, standing back up. He looked down at Max. "She's gone, and she's never coming back. I'm sorry."

Joel pointed the shotgun at the ground behind the truck. A thunderous blast echoed off the mountainside and throughout the tunnel.

"No!" the thing that looked like Max wailed. Its face contorted into something out of a horror movie, and its voice changed. "Why did you do that?"

"Joel?" a man's voice yelled from inside the tunnel.

The sheriff spun to his right and fired at the sound without hesitation, going against years of experience and training. I looked through the windshield and saw Walt standing there in a white button-up shirt and a black tie, looking like a real FBI agent. He stumbled backward as a red stain spread across his chest, and then he fell behind Joel's truck.

"Oh shit," Sheriff Potts said.

I looked back just in time to see the Max-thing run across the road like an animal on all fours and lunge at the sheriff. Sheriff Potts couldn't defend himself. Max landed on his chest and knocked him on his back. His pistol went flying out of his hand and slid somewhere under Joel's truck. I watched helplessly as Max put his hands on opposite sides of the sheriff's head and snapped his neck as easily as twisting the lid off a bottle.

"No!" Joel screamed and racked the shotgun.

"Oh my God," Dad said, still inside the car. He frantically crawled over to the driver's seat.

Joel looked past the creature still on top of the sheriff, then at my dad. "Get out of here, Roger!"

Dad tried to put the car in reverse, but it stalled out. The creature saw me in the back seat and smiled.

"Mav, your sister's in there." It nodded toward the tunnel. "Come get her. He's too much of a chickenshit," it said, gesturing toward my father in the front seat.

Dad turned around and spotted me.

"Jesus, Maverick!" He put it in reverse and whipped the car around until the mouth of the tunnel gaped behind us.

With no need to hide anymore, I sat all the way up and looked out the back window. I watched in horror as Joel put the tip of the shotgun to the side of the thing that used to be his son. A boom reverberated through the hills, startling Dad.

"Dear God, what is going on?" he said to himself as he floored the gas pedal.

Just before the gruesome scene disappeared from view, I watched as a translucent tentacle emerged from inside the tunnel like a giant squid feeling along the ocean depths. In one sweeping motion, it wrapped itself around the carnage. My stomach dropped as I saw how easily it crushed Joel's truck and pulled everything into the tunnel like a bunch of toppled bowling pins about to be reset. All the bodies—the evidence—disappeared into the abyss as we rounded the corner and fled back to Benson Drive.

PART SEVEN
THE HIDDEN

The official story of what happened that night to Joel, Walt, Sheriff Potts, and his deputies is a crock of shit. Don't get me wrong, though; to my knowledge, there was no cover-up or government conspiracy or anything like you'd see on The X-Files. The first responders who arrived at the tunnel the following morning discovered an accident, not a murder scene.

I've tried to tell myself for years that I didn't see what I saw when I looked back through the window of the sheriff's car. Even when I could block out the image of that tentacle that looked like it belonged to something from another dimension, I failed to erase what it actually did. The malevolent presence that dwelled within the slats of the tunnel had intentionally staged the aftermath. With one fell swoop, it managed to make every dead body and vehicle disappear. It sucked all the evidence into that black hole from whence it came.

As best as I can piece it together now, Walt had been parked on the other side of the tunnel. I know that because of what the incoming deputies had said over the car radio. I'm guessing that after Walt succeeded in his purpose of being a roadblock, he'd either driven his car into the tunnel once he heard the commotion on the other side or he'd walked through it. Either way, the creature in there had taken his car, too, leaving nothing for the sheriff's deputies to discover when they pulled up.

Now, as far as what happened to the lawmen who had the misfortune of working the graveyard shift that night, I can only offer conjecture. As I previously stated, the firefighters and the paramedics were responding to an automobile accident inside the tunnel.

A car full of high school seniors coming home from a kegger on the other side of town discovered a blazing inferno once they reached the entrance to the tunnel leading to Benson Valley, and they called 9-1-1. Three police cars from the county sheriff's department had seemingly crashed in the middle of the tunnel. The report states that the lead car had rounded the bend too fast and spun, lodging itself completely sideways. The cruiser behind it, car number two, T-boned car number one and then got rear-ended by car number three. Once one of the vehicles caught fire, that was enough to cause an explosive chain reaction. It was nothing like what Joel had originally planned, though. His dynamite never had a chance.

I've been told it was quite the ordeal for the firefighters to put out the burning pile of twisted metal before any serious damage could be done to the tunnel. There was none, of course. My only hope for the victims was that they all died on impact, but the nightmares tell me otherwise.

The visions that plague my dreams are close-up shots of the deputies, all trapped in their cars, hurt and badly mangled but not dead. The explosion was more of a fireball that spread from car to car, slowly cooking the screaming men alive as they watched each other char and melt onto their seats. I just don't see the tunnel having it any other way.

The only account of what truly happened rested with me and my dad. Had we been able to call someone and tell them, maybe things would've turned out differently, but that's not what happened. It would've been so much easier if we'd just gone home and called the state police or the FBI or the goddamn CIA while we were at it, but we didn't—we couldn't. If we'd managed to maintain possession of the sheriff's car that my dad used to make our getaway, we would've had some physical evidence to ground our outlandish testimony. All I know for sure is that I thought we had escaped as we fled back toward Benson Valley that night. I had no idea that the true horror was yet to come.

And now, as I sit here in Blake's childhood home, surrounded by unpacked moving boxes and a mattress on the living room floor, I'm documenting this account truthfully for the first time in my life. People need to know what happened in order to understand what I'm about to do. Or, hopefully, what I've already done if you're reading this right now.

Dad drove faster than I'd ever seen him drive before. He was normally the careful driver, the one mom had to tell, "Put some gas on it, pawpaw," when he drove a little too cautiously for her liking. But that was not the dad I got that night. I watched from the back seat of the sheriff's car as dark trees whizzed by my window. When I looked over Dad's shoulder, I saw the headlights shining on the asphalt zipping below us like a treadmill.

The speedometer displayed a readout of 84 mph as we neared the straight stretch that led to the train tracks marking the official entrance to Benson Valley. I looked back at the road just in time to see Jenny standing in the middle of it.

Dad slammed on the brakes. The back of the cruiser fish-tailed, and the smell of burnt rubber filled the interior of the car. Jenny didn't move. She just stood there on the faded yellow line of that country road and stared at us. My heart fluttered when I heard the handle on my dad's door click.

"Dad, what are you doing?"

He didn't even look back at me. His eyes were fixed on Jenny who stood there motionless, expressionless, a pale imitation of my sister if ever I'd seen one. He pushed the door open and stepped out.

"Jenny?"

I stared through the window as she slowly tilted her head to face him.

"Daddy?"

It wasn't her voice. Well, it was, but it sounded like a bad recording of my sister, not the real thing.

"Dad!" I slammed my hand on his seat.

He looked back at me.

"What, Mav? That's your sister!"

I could hear it in his tone that he didn't fully believe that statement. Tears filled my eyes even though I did my best to fight them off.

"It's not, Dad! It's just trying to trick you like Max tricked her—"

Dad shut the door, silencing my pleas. I panicked and tried to open my door even though every fiber of my being told me to stay in that seat. I jerked on the handle and pushed as hard as I could, but the door didn't budge. That's when it dawned on me:

I was in the back of a police car. The doors were designed to keep people who got arrested from getting out.

"Crap!"

I'd almost given up hope when I realized that there was nothing separating me from the front of the car. Despite what I'd seen in my favorite cop movies, there wasn't a partition of some clear, bulletproof material. There was, however, a mounted roll of mesh on the passenger side of the car. I looked at the opposite side and saw a lock and a latch for it to adhere to. For whatever reason, Sheriff Potts hadn't hooked up the protective divider that night.

Just as I started to climb between the two front seats, someone tapped on the rear window to my right. I turned my head and saw Jill standing there. She had the same blank expression on her face.

How is she here? Where is Mom?

And then another terrifying realization sank in: Jenny still had control of Jill. Jenny, who had been lured into the tunnel by Max and taken over by God-knows-what, was using the one sister I had left as a puppet.

I looked through the windshield as Dad continued to walk toward Jenny. Both twins still had on their matching white nightgowns that gave them an eerie, ghostlike glow. Jill's watchdog eyes trailed me as I climbed over the driver's seat. She took a sidestep and now watched me through the front passenger window.

"Jill?" I asked, but I knew the effort was futile.

A smile crept over her face as she slowly shook her head. In the darkness of her pupils, I knew that whatever lurked inside the tunnel enjoyed watching me squirm. The only thing I could think of was that Jill was here to prevent me from doing whatever Jenny wanted to do with Dad. I had to intervene.

I broke my gaze with her and climbed out of the car as quickly as I could. I knew she'd be coming for me. I'd never been physically afraid of my little sister until that point. My plan wasn't the greatest, but it was the first thing that came to mind.

"Dad, Jill is here!"

Dad turned around, looked at me pointing at Jill on the other side of the car, and then saw his other daughter.

"Daddy!" both sisters said at the same time, in the same voice. "Help us."

I watched as Jill turned from me and walked toward Dad. Jenny, too, slowly closed in on him. Dad's bewildered face was enough to give me hope that maybe he wasn't falling into this trap.

"Dad!" I shouted over them. "That's not the real Jenny."

The girls whipped their heads toward me, and in one monstrous voice said, "Shut your fucking mouth!"

Jenny's eyes began to glow as her breathing intensified. She leaned forward like an animal about to pounce on its prey.

Dad slowly backed away, saying, "No, no, no."

I could hear the loss in his voice, but more importantly, the acceptance. It sounds harsh reflecting back on it now, but I had to frame the next statement in a "good news/bad news" proposal.

"Jenny's gone. She's in the tunnel, and she's not coming back. Joel knew that. Why do you think he didn't believe Max back there? He told me what happened to his wife . . . how the tunnel wants to trick people—"

Jenny's burning eyes locked on me. "Shut your fucking mouth, you insignificant, meaningless piece of human shit!"

I immediately noticed that the voice only came from Jenny. When I looked at Jill, her eyes fluttered as she struggled to stay standing. Whatever had a hold of her was losing its grip. Dad saw it too. I pointed at my real sister again.

"She is still Jill, but that thing is not Jenny."

Dad's head darted between his two daughters. I can't imagine what kind of willpower it took for him to do what he did—how hard that decision must've been to abandon the last strand of hope that his daughter was still alive—but he forced himself into action. He turned his back to Jenny and ran toward Jill.

The beast in Jenny snarled and spasmed. Her fingers turned to gnarled claws as she arched her back and hissed. I knew what she—it—was about to do. That thing was going to kill my dad.

Fortunately, this was the same dad who'd let me steer his car on his lap when I was younger and who'd encouraged me to drive his car around empty parking lots. He used to say, "It's never too early to learn."

I jumped back into the car, put the gearshift in drive, and floored the gas pedal. The vehicle Dad had let me practice with was definitely not a souped-up police cruiser.

As soon as I pressed my foot down, my head sank into the headrest as I accelerated toward the demonic entity masquerading as my sister. The look on its baffled face probably matched mine as I shot forward in what felt like a roller-coaster. The Jenny-thing didn't have time to move. I closed my eyes for a split second to avoid seeing the inevitable impact. Feeling the car hit and then run over the body like a speed bump is something I'll never forget.

As soon as I opened my eyes, I slammed on the brakes and put the car back in park. My hands shook as I slowly released my grip on the steering wheel. I thought my heart was going to explode, but I took a deep breath and turned around.

The broken body of the creature stirred in the road. Its torso had been twisted completely backward at the waist. One of its legs had been severed at the knee and a substance like black tar pumped out of the stump. I winced as I watched its claws scratch against the asphalt until they snapped from its fingers. Its neck, now bent at a right angle, began to bloat like a water hose with a kink in it. The thing's once burning eyes were now black and glared into the depths of my soul.

Just when I felt like I was going to soil myself, it opened its mouth, and a geyser of that black liquid shot all over the road like a whale blowing out seawater.

And with that final belch, the carcass of the tunnel creature began to evaporate into the atmosphere like burning paper. It was only at this point that I felt safe getting out of the car.

I stepped onto the road and looked past the gruesome site at my dad, who'd been watching it too. His mouth hung open. Having just witnessed exactly what Joel had described happening to Darla's body years ago, I was slightly less baffled.

I know now that I felt relief more than anything. The worst thing that could've happened would've been for me to turn around after plowing through Jenny and see her mutilated corpse, not some otherworldly creature.

"Dad," I said.

He looked up, still speechless. Behind him, Jill stumbled and collapsed onto the ground beside the road. He turned and ran to her. By the time I reached them, Dad was bent over Jill, saying her name and rubbing her cheek. I stood next to him and watched as her eyelids fluttered open.

"Jill, baby, are you okay?"

She finally found my dad's face as she came out of the delirium.

"Daddy?"

It was her voice, all hers.

"Yes, it's me." He scooped her up and cradled her against his chest. "Let's get you home."

"Where are we?"

"Bad dream," Dad said, still sounding winded and shook up. "It's just a bad dream."

I followed him as he carried her down the road to the sheriff's car. He didn't say anything, and I didn't know what to say. One thing I did notice was how he never averted his gaze from the car. Not once did he look down at the black spot on the road that was still withering into the sky like soot caught in a breeze. He stopped at the door behind his. He didn't need to tell me what to do. I opened it, and he gently placed Jill on the back seat. I climbed in and scooted beside her. She leaned her head against my shoulder, still a bit out of it.

"It's okay," I said and put my arm around her.

Dad got in the driver's seat and shut the door. He started the car but didn't do anything but grip the wheel.

"Dad?" I began.

"What are we . . . What's going on?" He let out a hysterical chuckle and a whimper before rubbing his eyes. "Why haven't we seen any other cars? What is this?" he asked, shaking his head.

Seeing the man I'd looked up to my whole life—the most levelheaded guy who always had an answer for everything—reduced to someone so helpless and clueless scared me more than anything else up to that point.

"We need to go home to Mom," I said.

Dad took a deep breath and nodded his head.

"You're right. Everything's going to be okay."

It sounded like he was trying to convince himself more than us at that point. Just when he was about to take off, the police radio let out a screech that caused me and Jill to immediately cover our ears. Dad's whole body jolted. He snatched the staticky device off its base and held down a button on the side. The sound stopped, and Jill and I removed our hands.

"Hello? Is anyone there?" he asked.

As soon as he released the button, the loud screeching returned. We recoiled and covered our ears. Dad pressed the button again.

"Hello? Someone help us. If you can hear me, we need help—"

But something on the other end cut him off.

"No one is going to help you," a deep, guttural voice said.

Dad pulled the radio away from his face, staring at it like it was something alien. The screeching had stopped, but now an eerie humming came through. I wanted to believe it was just distorted radio waves, but the humming turned into a taunting, mechanical chuckle.

"Come back," it whispered. "Come back. Come back. Come back." With each plea, it changed voices like a symphony of tortured souls. "Come back. Come back. Come back."

"Turn it off, Daddy," Jill said. She was crying, and I hadn't even noticed.

"COME BACK!"

The monstrous voice was so loud and distorted that it vibrated the car. All the windows simultaneously exploded outward onto the street.

"Jesus Christ!" Dad said. He turned around and looked at us.

Jill's face was buried in my shirt, and I held onto her, doing my best to protect her.

"Are you all hurt?" he asked.

I looked at Jill and saw no injury. All of the glass had blown outside. Physically, we were okay.

"No," I said.

Jill still didn't look up or release her grip on me.

"We're getting the hell out of here," he said and turned back around.

Thank God.

As we drove the rest of the way, I did my best to guard my only sister from the onslaught of air rushing through the front of the car where the windshield used to be. Dad was driving half the speed he was when we first fled the tunnel, but with no windows protecting us from the elements, it felt like we were going a hundred miles per hour. Fortunately, we didn't have very far to go.

When we pulled into our driveway a few minutes later, I waited for my mom to emerge from the front door, but she never did. There was no sign of her. I thought maybe Jill had snuck out and Mom had gone looking for her. Dad killed the engine, got out, and opened my door.

"Be careful getting out. There might be glass."

I scooted across the seat with Jill still clinging to me.

"Come on, Jill," Dad said, picking her up. He looked at me. "Let's get inside to your mother."

I followed them into the house and walked straight into my dad's back. He'd stopped, and I didn't know why until I peered around him. Mom was lying on the living room floor with the remains of a shattered porcelain lamp beside her bleeding head.

"Jesus," Dad said and stood Jill beside me. He hurried and crouched next to Mom. "Leah?"

Mom's eyes opened, and she instantly winced. I took a few

steps into the room, making sure to keep Jill behind me. Dad helped her slowly sit up.

"What happened?" she asked.

I knew what happened, but I couldn't say it. Jill had obviously been under the control of that thing in the tunnel via Jenny and knocked Mom out with the lamp. That's how she was able to sneak out and meet us on the road.

"You have a slight gash on your forehead. You'll need stitches."

"Did I do that?" Jill asked.

Everyone turned to look at her.

"No," Dad said before anyone else had a chance to respond. "It wasn't you, baby."

"But I remember doing it. I couldn't help it. I'm sorry. Am I in trouble?" Jill started to cry.

Mom looked back and forth at us like we all knew something she didn't and was just figuring it out.

"Jenny," she said. "Jenny and Max . . . Roger, what's going on? Did you find them?"

She looked us up and down and then at my dad. I saw the tears form in her eyes.

"Jenny's gone," Dad said.

Mom sobbed as her body heaved with her heavy breaths. I ran over to her and hugged her. It was the only thing I knew to do. She squeezed me so tightly it hurt, but I didn't have it in me to break the embrace.

"How . . . how do you know?" she asked between sobs.

"I saw it with my own eyes, Leah. There's something I can't explain happening right now. We need to lock the doors and call for help."

Mom finally released me and looked at Dad like he'd just

said something so outlandish that she had to watch the words come out of his mouth to be believed.

"What do you mean, you saw it with your own eyes? What did you see, Roger?"

Dad and I briefly made eye contact, and in that moment, I felt like I'd dipped my toe in the land of the grown-ups. I know now that he looked at me with vulnerability, like a confidant and not a son from whom he had to keep the harsh secrets of the adult world.

I'd witnessed the same unbelievable sights he just had, and thinking back on it, I'd go so far as to say that if I hadn't acted when Dad was approaching Jenny in the middle of the road, she would've escorted him into the tunnel. Maybe, just maybe, Dad knew that I had, in fact, saved the day. Yes, I just officially turned a year older, but the way Dad shared this look with me was more of a validation than some arbitrary birthday.

"Let's get you up, and we'll talk," he said.

"Where's my daughter, Roger?" Mom cried as she got to her feet. "Where's my little girl?"

Dad took her by the shoulders and pulled her in for a hug. He glanced at me.

"Mav, lock the door and turn off the lights. We're all going to our room."

I followed Dad as he helped Mom down the hall. I had to grab Jill by the shoulders and redirect her from walking into the wall. We entered our parents' room, lit up by a small lamp on the nightstand on my mom's side of the bed. Dad helped Mom sit at the foot of the bed and sat down beside her. He looked at us and patted the empty mattress space on the other side of him.

"Come up here," he said.

Jill climbed up and curled into him. I moved Mom's pillow and wedged myself in.

Dad reached over and turned off the lamp beside the bed. The room went dark except for the moonlight shining in through the sliding glass doors. I thought about hopping off and walking over there to sneak a peek at my room across the courtyard, just out of curiosity, but I remained planted.

"Roger, tell me what's going on," Mom said with the posture of a deflated balloon and sounding a bit delirious.

"I'm not going to lie, Leah. I have no idea. All I know is there's something in that tunnel, something evil. It killed Max, Joel, Sheriff Potts, Walt . . . and Jenny."

"Jenny is dead, Daddy?" Jill asked in that high-pitched, on-the-verge-of-crying tone.

Dad wrapped his arm around her.

"Yes, baby. I'm so sorry."

My mom lost it and just kept repeating, "Oh my God," and crying. I felt bad for Dad, having to comfort both Mom and Jill on each side of him.

"Mav," he said, holding back his own tears.

"Yeah?"

"Why don't you take Jill and run a bath for her? I need to tell your mother what happened and call the state police."

"I don't want to take a bath," she said.

"You need one," I said. "You're covered in dirt."

"How can I take a bath in the dark?"

"Come on. It'll be fun," I said, standing up and taking her by the hand.

"Go ahead and lock the bedroom door, too," he said.

I followed orders and then led my sister to the "big bath-tub," as we called it. Even though the bathroom area was in the same wing of the house, a retractable partition wall separated it from the bedroom.

Back then, my parents had one of those whirlpool tubs encased in a rectangle of wood with two steps you had to climb to get in. There was even a rounded seat inside that we used to sit on once the water filled all the way up. Taking a bath in the big bathtub was a rare treat, so even after all she'd been through, Jill perked up at the idea. She began to undress when I started the water. Once the temperature was just right, I told her to get in and then crept back to the partition to listen to my parents.

Their voices were slightly muffled by the running water, but I heard bits and pieces of Dad's testimony, followed by intermittent gasps from Mom. She then cleared her throat and said, "We also need to call Brandy and tell her about Walt."

"The phone line's dead."

I tilted my head so that my ear pressed against the partition; I had to make sure I heard that correctly. What I had inadvertently done was angle my face at the sliding glass door. My blood ran cold when I looked into the courtyard.

"I know why the phone's dead," I said just loud enough for them to hear.

The mattress squeaked like it always did when Dad climbed off it. I listened to him walk to the partition opening. He poked his head around the corner and said, "What, Mav?"

All I could do was point. Dad followed my finger and looked through the sliding glass door at three moonlit figures standing in the courtyard: Walt, Brandy, and Blake.

PART EIGHT
THE ULTIMATUM

The tunnel still cuts through that corner of the hill to this day. Lights have been added to the interior so it's no longer a pitch-black C-shaped corridor. You don't have to turn on your head-lights when you drive through it. Another substantial upgrade is the stoplight they've installed on both sides. Gone are the days of coming to a slow crawl as you roll the windows down and listen for a honking automobile making its way through until it's your turn to start honking and flashing your lights.

They even gave the tunnel a name. I noticed that right away when I drove the U-Haul up to it on moving day. A bronze plaque was pinned front and center with the words HILLS-BURY TUNNEL printed on it. Naming it after the county seemed appropriate enough, though I have to admit that I initially read it as HELLSBURY TUNNEL.

I stopped at the red light hanging on the aged wooden front of the arched entrance. The fears I had as I made my way back to that very spot were assuaged as I viewed it from an adult perspective. It no longer resembled a giant gaping mouth like the poster for the movie Jaws. In fact, it seemed relatively small. As the years passed, my memory had stretched it out, making it taller and wider than it was in reality, or at least kept it over-sized like my childhood mind had registered it.

No cars came out as I patiently waited for my turn, but once that light turned green, all the fears of my youth came back with the flip of a switch. I had to drive into the mouth of madness. For a moment, I just sat there with my foot on the brake pedal. My eyes drifted from the glowing green light to the dark opening below it. And even though lights hung every twenty feet or so, patches of darkness still existed in there. I wondered if I hit the gas and entered the damned place, if one of those dark spots would open up, or if all the lights would suddenly shut off, leaving me alone in the middle of the C-shaped Hell for the creature inside to finally get me.

The honk of the car on my bumper jolted me out of hesitation. I looked in the side mirror and saw a red sports car, and my heart skipped a beat. My mind flashed back to the night when I turned thirteen and Max disappeared into the slats just as a red sports car whooshed through.

The redness.

I studied the driver and saw it was just some punk teenager behind the wheel. The bass from some shitty new excuse for a rap song thumped as he held up his arm like, What the hell, bro?

I turned away and literally faced my fears. Driving through with this red car behind me was the test to see if we'd truly ended it that night. Instead of thinking of what could go wrong, I remembered everything that happened to the people I loved that summer and in the years that had passed. A fury filled my being as I realized that, yes, I had survived, but my life had been taken from me. That fucking tunnel was both directly and indirectly responsible for so many family members and friends dying, the resulting trauma rippling exponentially through the lives of all the survivors.

I lifted my foot off the brake and floored the gas pedal, accelerating with all the speed of a gimp tortoise in that U-Haul, but the engine was sure loud enough. The sound of the revved-up motor echoed throughout the tunnel as I barreled through. The new lights stayed on, providing me with a clear view the whole way. Other than the jerkoff kid bumping his music behind me, there was no other sign of life. Still, a wave of relief washed over me when I saw the daylight ahead as I rounded the curve and approached the exit.

Just when I was feeling like I'd made it through unscathed, a cold sensation crept over me. It took less than a second to realize why; I was driving past the part of the tunnel where Max had disappeared. As I sped through, if I would only peek out the passenger window, I would be looking at the slats that served as the doorway to the darkness beyond all comprehension—the horrors that had held hostage my dreams and beckoned me back like some sinister siren singing for a lonely sailor.

I couldn't do it, though. I kept my eyes focused on the light at the end of the tunnel until I safely drove back into the sunlit world. Something, however, did come over me right as I made it out. A morbid curiosity caused me to look at the passenger side mirror, and I nearly swerved off the road. Just beyond the red car that was still riding my bumper, a pale figure as white and luminescent as the moon slowly withdrew back into the slats. I looked away as fast as I could, and despite not seeing any features on its amorphic face, I had the strangest sensation that it was smiling.

As I drove to my new home—Blake's old house—I wondered if I'd just made the biggest mistake of my life. Cruising along that old familiar road that still had most of the older houses and some new ones and passing a gaudy sign that read GOLDEN CIRCLE, I realized that I didn't have much of a life to waste anyway. If the last thing I did on this planet resulted in me bringing that creature's existence to an end, then I'd chalk that up as a victory.

Now, getting everything ready for what I know needs to be done, I'm more sure than ever that I'm doing something that could save and avenge countless lives . . . or I've gone completely insane. If my mission is successful, and you're reading this now, I don't know that you'll know the difference either.

I thought seeing my dead sister reincarnated into some creature from another dimension would be the scariest thing I'd witness that night, but when I looked out that sliding glass door at Walt, Brandy, and Blake, I felt sheer doom.

"That's not possible," Dad said.

"What is it, Roger?" Mom asked and peeked around the corner. "Is that . . . What are they doing here?"

I jumped at the sound of the metal rings scraping against the curtain rod when Dad yanked it shut. He made sure the door was locked and that it had the extra measure of the wooden stick wedged in the door track. "You all get back," Dad said to me and Mom, but neither of us listened. "Get away from the windows. Mav, turn off her water."

Before I could tell him that he'd just told me to start her bath, I thought better of it and hurried to do as I was told. Jill sat in the big bathtub with the water running. She had her back to us and splashed around as shampoo bubbles formed all around her. I gripped both knobs and twisted them to the right.

"Hey," Jill said. "That's not enough water. I want—"

"Shh," I said. "You have to be quiet right now."

"Is the bad man here?"

The question stung me. Which "bad man" was she referring to? Was there more than one or only one? She had been temporarily tethered to Jenny. Maybe she caught a glimpse of the true form of the horror that lived in the tunnel. Before I could answer her, someone knocked on the glass door.

Mom hurried around to our side of the partition and over to the bathtub. She grabbed a towel and pulled Jill out of the water.

"Let's get you dried off," she said and rubbed the towel over my sister in record time. She put one of her own small T-shirts on Jill, which covered her like a dress.

I looked at the shadow standing on the other side of the door. It was definitely Walt. It knocked again. I watched Dad carefully slide Mom's closet door open and withdraw a big wooden baseball bat. He left the door open and looked at Mom.

"You have to hide with them."

"No, are you crazy? We have to run," Mom said.

"We don't know what's out there, Leah. Protect them. We're out of options."

"I'm staying with you," I said.

Dad looked me up and down. I got the sense that he realized I actually could help him if it came down to it.

The figure knocked again and said, "Roger? It's Walt. I need you to let me in. I can explain everything."

131

Dad didn't even acknowledge the intruder outside. He homed in on Mom and said, "Please, just sit in there with Jill." And then he said even quieter, "She doesn't need to see what's about to happen."

Mom closed her eyes and gritted her teeth. She wasn't the hiding type, and I knew she was only going to do it because Jill was with us.

"Come here, baby. Let's hide in Mommy's closet." She looked at Dad with an intensity I'd never seen before. "Do your part out here."

It was obvious that she'd just caught him off guard. He'd either just been emasculated, motivated, or, most likely, a combination of both. Mom was normally the more assertive one of the two. I know now that it must've killed her, being reduced to hiding in a closet with one daughter dead and the people responsible standing on the other side of the glass door.

Once they were inside, Dad slid the door shut. He hurried over to the sink like he was looking for something. He scanned the corner where the toilet was but didn't find anything there either.

"Dad," I whispered. "What are you doing?"

He didn't respond. He just continued his frantic search.

"Roger, is Mav in there with you?" Walt's silhouette asked. "I have Blake with me. Blake, come here and say something."

There was something off about Walt's voice. It had an uncanny quality of something trying its best to mimic Blake's dad, but every third word or so would become distorted and deeper, more guttural.

The sound of the medicine cabinet opening made me turn back to Dad. He took something from the top shelf, shut the door, then crept over to me.

"Here. Take this."

I opened my hand and felt something metal and sharp. Before I could ask him what it was, he said, "If anything gets close to you, jam this in its belly as many times as you can."

When I felt the plastic handle on one end and the grooved metal that stretched about four inches until it formed a point, I knew he had handed me my mom's nail file as a weapon of last resort. I felt like Peter Pan with a little dagger about to take on Captain Hook with his hook and sword.

"Mav? Hey man, are you in there?"

I perked up. That was Blake's voice. It wasn't some monstrous imitation of him. That was really my friend out there. So why was he with Walt? I watched Walt get shot and pulled into that tunnel. Against all rational judgement, I asked, "Blake, what's going on?"

My father had never laid a hand on me and wouldn't for the rest of his life, but in that moment, he was reacting on sheer instinct. He grabbed me by the cheeks, completely covering my mouth, and squeezed.

"What the fuck are you doing?" he whisper-yelled.

I pulled back and broke free. Right then, my dad was the only person I wanted to stab with the nail file.

"They're not going to go away. And that's really Blake. He's in trouble. We have to do something."

I couldn't believe it. Had I not just saved our lives back at the tunnel? And here he was, treating me like a dumb kid again. I'd had enough.

"Look, I know more about what's going on than you do. Joel told me some pretty messed up stuff. Walt is one of them now. He's trying to get us to go into the tunnel."

Dad kneeled down, got right in my face, and said, "And what makes you think he hasn't taken his wife and son there already, huh?"

Before I could say anything about how that wasn't physically possible because he would've been on foot since we drove the police car here, Blake said with a tearful voice, "Mav, if you don't let us in, Dad's gonna kill Mom and me."

Another shadow approached the curtains, this one shorter than Walt but bigger than Blake. It had to be Brandy.

"Please, Roger. Please just at least open the curtain, for Christ's sake," Brandy said, sounding even more upset than Blake.

"Dad, she's normal too."

Dad looked down at me and slowly nodded his head. He grabbed the curtain and pulled it back.

"Oh shit," he said.

The three of them stood a few feet away from the door in the courtyard. Walt was in the middle with Brandy on his right and Blake to his left. He held a black pistol in his hand and had it pressed to the back of Brandy's head. His other hand gripped Blake's shoulder, as if making sure neither of them were going anywhere.

Dad approached the glass and looked at the horrified faces of the two hostages.

"What do you want, Walt?"

"It's not what I want, Roger. It's what we all want, right?"

"I don't want this. What do you mean?"

The whole time the two of them were talking, Blake and I stared at each other. His puffy red eyes suggested that he'd been crying hard nonstop. I noticed that his swollen lower lip had a bloody crack in the middle like he'd been hit with the butt of a gun. I examined his mom's face and detected a black eye. My heart sank when I saw the dark red handprints around her neck. Somehow, Walt had made it back to his house and violently abducted his family.

I couldn't imagine the terror they must've felt, seeing this version of Walt burst into each bedroom and do God-knows-what to get them out of the house. They knew nothing about what had happened with the tunnel that night. If I was in Blake's shoes, I would've assumed my dad had just flipped his shit like Jack Nicholson in The Shining, another one of our favorite movies that I proudly displayed on my VHS rack, even though Max didn't have the patience for it. He always thought it was too slow.

Walt grinned, and that black liquid dribbled down his chin. It wasn't as thick, probably because it was mixed with his saliva. It had the consistency of runny watercolor paint compared to the tar that came out of Jenny.

"They're still in the tunnel," the Walt-thing said. "Your little girl, Joel, Darla, the sheriff, Max . . . they're all still in there. They're just trapped between worlds like I was when it took me in."

"I don't know what's happening," Dad said, "but I do know that my daughter is gone. I saw it with my own eyes."

"Yeah," I said, stepping up to the glass. "You can't trick us. You're not Walt. You're . . . Well, I don't know what you are, but you're not one of us!"

Walt frowned, looking genuinely upset by my remark.

"Why, sure I am, Mav. Do you think just because you ran that thing over in the street that Jenny is gone for good? Malarkey. She was a clone. A copy pieced together by the ancient one in the tunnel. Jenny is still in there with it, but she needs you to come and get her. That's the rule. I'm taking my family back to it so they can be like me, so they can see what I see. There are worlds beyond this one, and they are glorious."

"Don't take them," Dad said. "If there's any part of you in

there, Walt, please, don't take them. Drop the gun and go back yourself if it's so wonderful."

The creature inside Walt laughed like it had lungs full of muck.

"We're way past that now."

Recalling what the xeroxed copy of Max had told me earlier, I said, "But you can't do that! Everyone has to go willingly. That's the rule!"

"You know," Walt began, "you're right, Mav. Here, watch this." He took the gun away from Brandy's head and shoved it in Blake's mouth. Blake's eyes opened wide.

"No!" Brandy screamed and tried to reach for the gun, but Walt grabbed a handful of her hair and jerked her head back.

"Brandy, my dear, do you want to go into the tunnel with me and see sights that have to be seen to be believed?"

Brandy winced and cried. Walt pressed the gun further into Blake's mouth, causing him to choke.

"Yes!" she said. "Yes, I'll go, Walter, just please don't hurt our boy."

Walt pulled the gun back out of Blake's mouth. He gagged, and I thought he was going to barf right there.

"You sick son of a bitch!" Dad pounded the window with the bottom of his fist.

"Oh, I'm not finished yet," Walt said. "Mav wanted to make sure I'm following the rules." He looked at Blake. "Son, will you go with your mother and father into the tunnel?"

Blake swallowed and seemed to regain his composure. He looked at Walt, who pointed the gun at Brandy's temple, and then he looked at me through the glass. I shook my head.

After a moment, Blake said, "No."

Walt's eyes darkened into two black holes. "I'm sorry. What

was that?" He pressed the gun into Brandy's temple, causing her to wince.

"I said I'm not going into the fucking tunnel!"

Walt pulled the gun away from Brandy and shot Blake in the back of the head. Blood and bone sprayed the glass in front of my face.

Everything happened so fast. Brandy wailed a painful sound that only the loss of a child could elicit. Dad and I both stood in shocked silence. I heard Mom say, "Oh my God. Oh my God," from the closet while trying to comfort Jill.

Brandy swung her fists at Walt, beating his face mercilessly as he stood there and took it like he couldn't feel a thing, which, thinking back on it, he probably couldn't. Walt finally grabbed both of her wrists and said, "It's okay, baby. It's okay. Shh. We're taking him with us. We can bring him back. Do you want him to come back? Do you really want to go now? Huh?"

Brandy dropped to her knees and crawled over to her dead son with the exit wound that had blown out the front of his face like a bloody, blooming rose. She held his corpse in her lap and sobbed.

"Are you really ready to go now?" Walt asked, laughing.

"Yes! Just bring my baby back, please!"

"Yahtzee! That's what I wanted to hear!"

Dad and I still just watched the horror show unfold. I finally snapped out of it and pulled the dowel out of the door track. Dad was in shock, not even paying attention to what I was doing until he heard the click of the lock on the door. He looked at me just as I slung it open.

"Maverick!" he yelled, but I jumped through the opening. I threw the piece of wood at Walt. He swatted it away easily like I knew he would. While his hands were up, I stabbed his gut with the nail file, wiggling it back and forth.

I withdrew the blade and a black liquid like octopus ink squirted on my forearm. Walt grunted but didn't seem too affected. I plunged the blade into the side of his throat. The metal snapped from the handle and stayed stuck in his neck, making him look like the stereotypical version of Frankenstein's monster, minus one neck bolt. He dropped the gun and felt for the foreign object embedded in the tender flesh.

Walt gargled when he tried to say something, but Dad cracked his skull with the baseball bat. He stumbled backward as the black ooze shot out of his neck in pulsating globs. The side of his head where Dad hit him was slightly caved in, but Walt remained on his feet. Dad took another step toward him and raised the bat to deal a death blow.

"Stop!" Brandy ordered.

Dad looked over his shoulder at her. She'd picked up Walt's gun and had it pointed at him.

"Don't kill him. He has to bring Blake back."

Dad didn't move. Walt continued to stumble around, not a threat at that moment.

"What are you doing?" I asked. "That's not how this works."

Brandy looked back and forth between me and Dad. I got the feeling that she was at least willing to hear me out.

"If you let him take Blake into the tunnel to those monsters, they're not going to magically fix him and give him back to you," I said as I started to cry. "Blake is dead, and if he goes into the tunnel, he'll come out even worse."

Brandy seemed to think this over and concluded rather quickly. She had resolved whatever internal conflict plagued her, judging by the suddenly numb expression on her face.

"I can't live without my boy." She put the gun to her head and pulled the trigger.

"No!" Dad yelled before her body even hit the ground.

The gun cartwheeled across the courtyard and rested at Walt's foot. Even though he looked like he could keel over at any moment, he bent down and grabbed the firearm before my dad could take another swing at him. Dad froze as he stared at the monster that looked like it was dying to pull the trigger.

"Now . . ." Walt said, struggling to speak with the blade still in his neck. "It looks like . . . I'm going to need you . . . to drive."

"I'm not going with you," Dad said.

Even though Walt's eyes were still completely black, I could see that he rolled them. He swung the gun in my direction.

"Do I . . . need to go through . . . all this again?"

"Fine. Fine. I'll drive."

"Good," Walt said, keeping the weapon on me. "Start by putting them . . . in the trunk . . . of the sheriff's car."

Dad gave him a perplexed look.

"Now," Walt said.

I watched Dad swallow his emotions as he bent over and lifted Blake's corpse. He looked at me and said, "It's going to be okay."

I nodded even though I knew it was bullshit. Nothing would ever be okay again. Dad disappeared around the side of the house, leaving me face-to-face with the leaking Walt-thing that just stared and grinned at me until Dad returned. Dad didn't say anything as he squatted down and lifted Brandy's body the same way. Again, he passed by me and gave me a nod that I'm sure was meant to be reassuring but did nothing to lift my spirits.

"Are you going in . . . willingly . . . Mav?" Walt asked.

I had already made up my mind when that bastard shot Blake.

"Of course," I said. I didn't care if I died or not. I just wanted a chance to kill whatever cowardly creature lived in the darkness of those slats.

"Atta boy."

Dad walked back around with the keys in his hand.

"Okay, let's go," he said, speaking only to Walt.

"Everyone . . . is going."

"What?" Dad said, trying to sound angry, but I only heard the fear.

"Get your wife . . . and daughter."

"What? No, that's not part of the deal."

"Mav's already . . . agreed to come," Walt said with a hideous grin as he pointed the gun at me again. "Wife and daughter . . . now."

Dad balled his fists and approached the open bedroom door. I listened as he opened the closet door and mumbled something to Mom. Moments later, Dad emerged carrying Jill who had her face buried in Dad's neck. Mom followed behind him. Her eyes widened when she saw all the blood in the moonlight and then gasped when she saw the ghastly embodiment of Walt.

"Shh," Walt said. "We don't want . . . to wake . . . the neighbors. We've been . . . loud enough . . . already." He tilted his head toward the gun, and I wondered why no neighbors had called the police, but then I realized that even if they had called in a report of gunshots in the neighborhood, nothing was getting through that tunnel. No help would be coming for us. If there was any chance of making it out of this, we'd have to do it ourselves. When my parents told me that becoming a teenager meant becoming more independent, this wasn't what I had in mind.

Walt gestured with the gun toward the side of the house and said to my dad, "Lead the way."

Dad crossed the yard carrying Jill in one arm and holding Mom's hand with his other, practically having to drag her as she kept turning back to glare at Walt. I walked of my own volition, step-by-step with my father, fueled by pure hatred and a bit delusional if I'm being honest, looking back on it now.

When we reached the police cruiser, Walt glared at me and said, "You get in first . . . then mama bear . . . then the little cub."

Mom went off.

"Fuck you! I'll kill you, you piece of shit! You killed my daughter!"

"And I'll kill the other one, too, you grotesque cunt, if you don't get in the fucking car right now," Walt said, pressing the gun against Jill's cheek.

I stood there, unsure of what to do, trying to figure out the method to his madness.

"Now!" Walt barked, causing a big shot of black neck juice to hit the driveway and send him into a coughing fit.

I got in first, then Mom, reluctantly, and then Jill. After cramming inside in the order he demanded, he said to Dad, "Now . . . you get us . . . to the tunnel." Walt stood beside the open rear door until Dad got in the driver's seat and shut the door. His monstrous head peered in and politely asked Jill to scoot over.

Mom pulled Jill close to her as Walt squeezed into the back seat and shut the door. Dad turned around and saw the gun pointed at Jill's head. Walt grinned and said, "Take us home."

Dad started the engine and drove Sheriff Potts's car back to the tunnel.

PART NINE
THE TETHERING

Jenny and Jill always had a connection, as I've stated before. The research I've studied since the summer of 1999 revealed that some twins seemed to be linked psychically, others to a greater extent, such as physiologically. When one gets a headache across the country, the other one feels the same symptoms. The polar end of the spectrum exists, as well. There are twins of all varieties that share no connection other than the time they spent in the womb together. This phenomenon has been explained scientifically and through parapsychology. Basically, whatever answer you're looking for on the internet is what you'll find.

Looking back on the incident at the tunnel now, it's hard not to see divine forces at work. Had my sisters not possessed this freakish bond they shared since birth, events would've played out much differently—of that, I'm sure.

I called Jill earlier today under the guise of "catching up." The reality of the situation is that I don't know if I'll ever get the chance to talk to her again. I also wanted to be one-hundred-percent sure that any connection to Jenny was severed on the final night at the tunnel.

As you can assume, this childhood memory wasn't something she cheerfully wanted to revisit when I broached the topic. I knew I had to tread lightly, so I segued the conversation by asking what she imagined Jenny would be doing had she not disappeared that summer. Jill paused, and for a moment I thought I had derailed the conversation. Out of nowhere, she just said that she knew Jenny would've grown up to be a veterinarian. We shared a laugh at how much she loved her stuffed animals and always carried around a bunny Beanie Baby.

I asked her how much she thought about Jenny, and surprisingly, she said not much anymore. Initially, she'd see her every time she looked in the mirror, but as time passed, so did the shadow of Jenny's presence.

It dawned on me during this conversation that we'd never had one like it before. Our coping mechanism was denial. The murders and monsters and mysteries surrounding that tunnel never happened. I know this was our mom's doing. After Dad killed himself, she did her best to make sure that what remained of her family stood a chance at a normal life, though that, in itself, was its own form of delusion. Once we went into the tunnel, literally and metaphorically, there would never be a "normal" for us.

Jill and I talked for almost an hour. Whenever I felt like she was wrapping up the conversation by her tone, I prodded a bit further. I had to be sure. After witnessing the power of their connection that night, I needed to know that there wasn't some lingering open line like me and Max with the walkie-talkies. If there existed a presence of that thing in the tunnel in my sister's mind because her other half disappeared into that abyss, then what I was planning on doing could be catastrophic.

Satisfied with her responses, I finally told her that I had work to do and that we should stay in touch because the conversation had been so pleasant. She invited me to come and spend some time with her and her family soon, and I even accepted.

It's a lovely thought, but as I sit here typing this confession, I don't know if it'll ever happen. I have no idea what to expect tonight. All I know is that I'm going to the tunnel with a plan— a modified, less risky version of Joel's. I have enough dynamite packed in the garage—acquired from a source I won't disclose —to level the cursed tunnel and the entire side of the mountain it cuts through. My efforts won't be thwarted by Sheriff Potts or my dad either. At least, I hope not. Christ, that's a terrifying notion I never thought about until right this minute. But I know something now that Joel didn't, and that's why my plan is better.

The common denominator for all the direct abductions that I know of is the color red. Darla had a red car when she disappeared; a red car passed through when Max got nabbed, plus he was riding a red bike. I only spotted the pale bastard in the rearview mirror because it came out right when the car behind me passed those slats. And then there was the flickering red police lights on Sheriff Potts's car from the night I thought we killed it.

This is the way to draw out what I'm now referring to as The Recluse, the creature trapped in the darkness that only emerges to drag people down to feast on and spits out doppelgängers to bring back more willing victims. I don't know how many people it's gotten over the years, nor the potentially catastrophic effect it could have or has had on us through its exponential infestation of our world.

When I said that my dad brought the apocalypse to our dinner table in the summer of 1999, I didn't realize the true meaning behind that statement. I do now, and it's why I have a red Ford Mustang filled with explosives parked in the garage, ready for a midnight ride.

Dad stopped the car well before the entrance to the tunnel. I watched from the back seat as he gripped and released the steering wheel several times like a stress ball. We all just sat in silence in the windowless vehicle, looking straight ahead at the arch of darkness that invited us in with no obvious threat of malice.

A light drizzle blew in through the broken windows and coated the black asphalt in front of us, still warm and sunbaked from the summer day. Mist rose up from the road, creating an eerie scene before the tunnel.

"Well? What now?" Dad asked. I could tell he was doing his best not to antagonize the ghoul holding his family hostage in the back seat.

"Ouffff—" Walt began to speak but barfed out a handful of that tar-like substance all over the back seat. A continuous stream trickled out of his neck wound. He coughed and gurgled and tried again. "Out . . . with the bodies, Roger."

Dad turned around and looked at us, probably making sure we were all still okay, then turned to Walt. "What do you mean?"

"Take . . . the bodies . . . out of the . . . fucking trunk!" Blood and more phlegm expelled from him when he spoke like a slobbery dog shaking its head.

"And do what with them, Walt?"

"Place them . . . in front of . . . the tunnel . . . nice and neat," Walt said with a smile and then another coughing fit.

For a moment, Dad looked unsure of what to do.

"Roger, just do it," Mom said so quickly that it startled me. She sounded agitated, like when she'd tell me to clean my room and I'd forget, and she'd come back to see I hadn't accomplished shit. It was Mom's angry tone that snapped everyone in line when she unleashed it.

"Okay." Dad opened the door and got out.

He made it three steps before Walt yelled, "Close the door!"

Dad jumped and turned around, looking at us through the open back window as he did as he was told. I watched him walk around to the back of the cruiser. As I followed him, I noticed Jill with her face still buried in Mom's chest, and Mom just staring straight ahead like she was the one holding the gun.

The car jostled as Dad popped open the trunk. I didn't want to picture what he was doing, and I felt so bad for him having to do it. Every little shake of the car reminded me that the corpses of my friend and his mom were getting shuffled around the back like luggage. I did my best to ignore the gurgling, wheezing sounds Walt produced in the dead silence.

Slightly turning my head toward him, I looked at the breathing corpse beside me. Just like Mom, he was fixated on the tunnel. I looked at the gun in his pale, bloated hand, resting on his leg. His attention wasn't on it. If I was fast enough, I knew I could get it. He'd be slow and shocked at my daring maneuver, and I'd shoot a hole through his face. If the blast was anything like what happened in the action movies I had seen, at this range, the bullet would go straight through his head and out the busted window behind him and ding the FALLING ROCK sign beside the car. An exit wound the size of a softball would be left in its wake. This would give us enough time to reach through the broken windows—which still had enough exposed shards to rip an arm to ribbons if it slid across one—and open the door from the outside, making our escape from the hellish prison.

I got us into this mess, and I'd be the one to get us out. Just as I took a deep breath before making my move, the car shook as Dad removed a body. He passed by Walt's open window with Brandy over his shoulder in a fireman's carry. Her arms and hair hung over his back, and her dead eyes passed by, causing my stomach to twist into knots. I swallowed and tried to mask my fear. All courage that I'd summoned for my abandoned rescue mission had abated.

Dad trudged toward the tunnel, lit up by the headlights that cast a massive shadow of him against the wooden front that shrunk as he neared the entrance. Even though it looked like he struggled to do it, Dad carefully maneuvered Brandy's body and placed it in the middle of the road, just where the light met the darkness. He folded her arms across her chest, probably out of respect or dignity or something, but it just made her look like a sleeping vampire to me. He turned around and walked back to the cruiser, shielding his eyes from the headlights shining directly in his face.

Walt emitted a sickening chuckle that sounded like a drowning man trying to laugh. Dad came around to Walt's side of the car, and the bleeding bastard gave him a nod of approval as he walked back to the trunk. Again, the cruiser rocked a bit as Dad took out the second body: Blake.

I jumped when he slammed the trunk and told myself I

wouldn't look this time. I'd watched Blake get shot and his face come apart right in front of me earlier; I had no desire to see what it looked like now. I averted my gaze to the tunnel and focused solely on that; however, what I saw there was no less terrifying.

One long deformed arm inched its way out of the darkness. The pale extremity crawled across Brandy's face and snaked its way down her body. I watched the alien-thing change shapes before my eyes. It started as an arm and then cracked and popped like it had several joints—an arm longer than the length of an entire human body with elbows every few feet, bending in different directions.

As if that weren't enough for my mind to process, in one quick spasm, it became a tentacle that could only belong to some ancient sea monster dwelling in the deepest ocean depths, accustomed to never seeing the sun. It was a smaller version of what I'd seen emerge from there previously. I blinked, and it curled around her like an anaconda with the speed of a lightning strike. Brandy was no more than some-thing entangled in a translucent, pulsating tentacle. And in one swift jerk, she was gone.

"Oh my God," I whispered.

"God? There is . . . no God," Walt said, enjoying the show.

I don't think Dad saw what had happened. He neared the front of the car, carrying Blake in his arms like a parent would carry a sleeping child to bed. Right as he neared the tunnel, he stopped and stared at the empty spot where he'd just placed Brandy. He turned around and squinted into the headlights like we would be able to provide him with an answer.

My skin prickled as two crooked arms scurried out of the tunnel, across the mist-covered road, and crawled up my father.

"Dad!" I screamed, but Walt backhanded the side of my face so hard that I fell on top of my sister.

When I looked up, I watched the tentacles snatch Blake's body from Dad's grasp. His thin body smacked on the pavement as the ghostly white snakes pulled him through the mist and into the tunnel.

"Dad, run!" I screamed and got pelted on the side of the head again. That son of a bitch got me good that time. My world spun and went dark, but I didn't lose total consciousness. I felt a struggle being fought over me. Walt grunted and coughed and cussed. I heard Mom giving it right back to him.

The heavy weight pressing down on my back had to be Walt. As I blinked the stars out of my eyes, I realized that I was staring at the floorboard in the back seat. I could see Jill's bare feet and Mom's slippers. Her legs were kicking like she was fighting to breathe. My elbow flew back with the force of a UFC fighter from one of Max's few VHS tapes that I'm pretty sure he either stole from 7-Eleven or rented and never returned.

Walt grunted, and the weight lifted off me. I rose quickly and saw the rage in the thing that barely resembled a living human. He stared at me with genuine shock that shifted to amusement, maybe even pride.

"All right, Walt. Don't you dare touch my fucking children," Mom said.

Baffled, I slowly turned to see that she held the gun and pointed it directly at Walt's decomposing face. Somehow in the struggle, she'd managed to wrangle it free. She made sure that Jill and I were not in the line of fire as she kept it locked on him. I like to think I aided in this turn of events with my vicious elbow attack, but I don't know for sure.

"Go ahead," Walt said. "Shoot."

Just when I thought Mom wasn't going to do it, Dad opened

the door behind her. It startled her so bad that she fired as she fell out of the car backward. I'd never heard a sound so loud in my life. Jill covered her ears, crying as she hid on the floorboard behind the driver's seat with her head tucked into her arms.

My ears were ringing. I couldn't imagine how loud it would've been if we had windows and a windshield to contain the sound. Walt's leg twitched against mine. I looked at him and saw the damage done. Had Mom fired straight on, it would've nailed him between the eyes. But since she shot him as she fell, the trajectory of the bullet struck him in the right side of his face, leaving him with a jaw hanging on by just a few strands of flesh.

Dad caught Mom as she fell and pulled her out like the car was on fire. He ran back and scooped up Jill, looked at me with a frantic intensity, and said, "Let's go!"

I took one last look at Walt who'd slumped back against the car door, struggling to keep what was left of his head from dangling out of the window.

"Now, Mav!"

I turned back around and leaped out of the car. For a moment, the four of us stood there by the cruiser, Jill still in Dad's arms as he glanced around like he was trying to figure out what to do.

The car beside us moved. I couldn't believe it. Walt's arms gripped the cruiser's bar of red and blue lights as he pulled himself out of the window and onto the top of the car and crouched, watching us like a wounded gorilla.

Mom aimed the gun and squeezed the trigger, but it was empty.

"Shit."

There was nothing human in what used to be Walt's eyes. They were a creamy white that glowed in the night. And although half his jaw dangled from his cheek flesh, a deep voice that made my bowels ache said, "You're not going anywhere."

"Leah, take the kids and run," Dad said, eyeballing the creature.

Walt smiled and shook its head.

"It needs more sacrifices," Walt said.

I stared at the paused body in front of me that was somehow communicating as clearly as ever. I knew we weren't speaking to Walt's doppelgänger. We were talking to the thing in the tunnel, The Recluse.

"I'm not going anywhere," Mom said. She had a tone like she wanted to leap onto the car herself and attack the thing.

Dad handed Jill to me without warning. I nearly dropped her but maintained my grip. Dad looked at me like he knew it would be for the last time and said, "Get her out of here and don't come back."

I wanted to cry, but I held it in and nodded my head, prepared to take off at a full sprint. Jill twitched in my arms. I glanced down to see her looking up at me with those same glowing eyes, but there was no malice in them.

"Mav?" she said, but it wasn't Jill. It was Jenny.

I know I've made a big deal out of how similar my twin sisters were, but they didn't look the same to me, even though they were identical. They only appeared that way to people who didn't see them all the time. They didn't sound the same to me. Their personalities were different, and they had separate tastes in food. I realized then, as I easily recognized Jenny's voice coming out of Jill's mouth, that they weren't an "it," as I had referred to them before. Jenny was Jenny, and Jill was Jill. My twin sisters were individuals.

"Jenny?" I whispered. "How? How are you here right now?"

But I knew the answer to the question as soon as I'd asked it. As much agency as each of my sisters possessed, they still had that bizarre connection. They were psychically tethered, and Jenny was taking full advantage of it to help us.

Walt sprung at Mom face-first, both arms reaching toward her like a jungle cat attacking its prey. Dad stepped directly in its path and wrapped his arms around Walt in midair. They both fell to the ground with a thud and rolled around. Dad ended up on top as the two of them came to a stop in the mist. I could barely see Walt in the rolling white wave. Mom ran over to them and kicked at what I assumed was Walt's head as Dad wrestled to keep it from squirming away.

"They're coming," Jenny said through Jill.

I looked down at her.

"Who?"

I watched as she turned her head and pointed at two mounds of mist crawling out of the tunnel.

"Them," she said.

I observed them flatten out and disappear, completely camouflaged. I froze at the realization of what they were and how quickly they'd become that way. Walt's hand shot out of the mist, grabbed Mom's ankle, and jerked her so hard that she fell on her back. Dad grabbed Walt's head and lifted it out of the fog, only to slam it back down on the pavement. He screamed in a rage and did it again. The thing that was Walt growled as its limbs spasmed up and down.

Mom struggled to stand as two figures emerged from the ground behind her. It was Brandy and Blake.

"Mom!" I screamed, pointing.

She looked at me and turned around, but it was too late. Brandy grabbed Mom's hair and pulled her back toward the tunnel.

"Roger!" she yelled, but when Dad looked up, Blake tackled him off Walt.

"Jenny, what do I do? What do I do?" I asked in a panic, unable to think, unable to move.

"Dad left the keys in the car," she said, pointing to Sheriff Potts's cruiser.

I hurried back to the car. I opened the back door and lay Jill on her side. Her body stayed in that paralyzed state, eyes still glowing. I got in the driver's seat as quickly as I could and started the engine.

"What are you doing, Mav?" Blake asked from outside.

I looked over and saw him standing in the middle of the road with his hands in the pockets of his gym shorts. There was something off about him. He stood at an awkward angle, and that's when I noticed that one leg was longer than the other because the kneecaps weren't parallel. I stared at his face and saw that it didn't match up either. His eyes were spaced about two inches farther apart than before, and his nose drooped down his face like it didn't have any cartilage in it. Whatever had created them didn't have the time to fully transform them into perfect copies. The presence in the tunnel needed two more bodies to get Mom and Dad off Walt, so it spat them out prematurely.

"Turn on the lights," Jenny said from the back.

I didn't know anything about the lights in the car. I twisted knobs and pulled a lever behind the wheel and red and blue lights spun and flashed across the side of the hill, and the high beams lit up the tunnel. Right where the road curved inside, I saw the black hole in the slats. The pale face of The Recluse stared back at me. My eyes widened at the hideous sight.

"Maverick, get out of here!" Dad screamed.

I broke from my trance and looked to my left to see that the bloody monstrosity that used to be Walt had its arms wrapped around my dad. Even though its head was a bloody pulp, it had the strength to lift him up and start walking to where Brandy restrained Mom in a choke hold.

"It doesn't have to be like this," Blake said. "I mean, look at me. I'm all better."

"You look like Mr. Potato Head," I said. "I don't know what you are, but you're not Blake."

I shifted into reverse.

"I wouldn't do that if I were you," he said.

His icy tone was enough to make me reconsider, and I kept my foot on the brake.

"My parents are going to kill yours if you don't go in," he said.

I felt my heart sink. I knew they could easily do it. Walt held Dad like a rag doll, and it looked like Mom was losing consciousness from being choked by the grinning thing that somewhat resembled Brandy. Her face was even more distorted than Blake's with her eyes close to her mouth, all under an extended forehead. She looked like someone poorly formed a human face out of modeling clay. I glared at Blake, and he smiled and said in a deep voice that wasn't his, "Everybody is going in."

"It's okay, Mav," Jenny whispered.

I gave my parents one more glance. Walt now held Dad with one arm wrapped around his chest and the other one gripping his jaw, sending me the message loud and clear that he would snap his neck if I didn't comply. Mom's eyes flickered as her oxygen supply continued to dwindle.

"Fine! I'll go! Just don't kill them." My heart was racing, and I felt my eyes start to water.

Blake smiled and said, "Good. Now get out. We have to convince your parents."

"Go, Mav," Jenny said.

I looked down so Blake couldn't see my mouth moving and said, "Go where? Are you crazy?"

"It's the red light. It draws it out."

"Come on," Blake said. "Let's go."

I raised my head and saw the pale silhouette of The Recluse watching with its white fingers wrapped around the slats, and all I felt was pure hatred. The hole from which it peered was growing larger like an oil leak with every rotation of the red light across its surface. It had reached the size of a soccer goal by then.

"Ghost ride it, Mav. Like you do with your bike," Jenny said, referring to when I would pull into our yard and hop off my bike without bothering to stop it, just to see how far it would roll on its own.

I looked in the rearview mirror at the open back window that had been blown out. That would be our escape.

"We can make it," Jenny said. "Go, now."

I shifted into drive and floored the cruiser, knowing exactly how much torque the engine had after having found out earlier. All I had to do was keep the wheel steady. The car was already perfectly lined up with the portal. As soon as the car breached the tunnel, I got up and dashed between the two seats. Jenny had already crawled halfway through the open back window. I grabbed under her shoulders and lifted as hard as I could, heaving her all the way out onto the trunk.

She looked at me with those glowing eyes and said, "Love you, Mav." Her eyes went back to being Jill's regular color, and I could tell that Jenny was gone, and my other sister was back in control. The front of the car nose-dived like it was going off a

156

cliff and smacked something that unleashed an otherworldly cry of pain and rage. Jill and I shot up like we were on the rising end of a seesaw. As I flew through the air, I watched the cruiser disappear into the abyss with the tentacled monster caught on the front of it. The car completely vanished from our plane of existence before we hit the ground.

I landed on my side, and Jill fell on top of me. It hurt like hell, but she wasn't crying and appeared uninjured. I turned to glimpse at the slats, expecting to see some kind of pissed-off monster crawling toward us. It was hard to see in the dark because our only light source had been Sheriff Potts's car, but I could barely see that the tunnel's side looked normal—nothing but wooden beams and gaps in between.

"Maverick!" Dad screamed from outside.

"We're okay!"

I helped Jill up.

"What happened?" she asked.

Two figures appeared at the opening of the tunnel: Mom and Dad. They were by themselves and held each other up as they walked.

"It's gone," I said as relief washed over me. "Come on. Let's get out of here." I took Jill by the hand, led her to our parents, and the four of us met in one big embrace.

Mom broke it up and began looking us over.

"Are you all okay? Are you hurt?"

"We're fine," I said. "What happened to Blake and Walt and Brandy?"

"They just . . . disappeared," Dad said as he nervously looked into the tunnel and surveyed the surrounding area.

"We should get out of here," Mom said through a strained throat that she rubbed.

I turned and looked at the tunnel that still looked like the same boring tunnel it always had been before the night we'd decided to sneak out and had the cosmic misfortune of colliding with the red car and The Recluse.

"It's okay. It's over," I said with a grin. "We killed it."

"How did you know to do that?" Mom asked.

I looked down at Jill who was waiting on my answer, too, letting me know that she had no memory of what Jenny had done.

"Jenny told me what to do," I said.

Mom covered her mouth with one hand.

"It's okay, Mom. She's free now."

Oh, how terribly wrong I was.

PART TEN
DEAD END

The world can be a beautiful place, one full of wonder, mystery, and majesty. From the ocean depths to the tips of the tallest mountains and everything in between, Earth is a dynamic planet, and that's not even factoring in humans and the agricultural, architectural, philosophical, and technological advances we've made, for better or worse. But one fatal flaw all humans possess is assuming that existence begins and ends with us.

What lies beyond the clouds and the outermost layer of our atmosphere is an endless expanse that is the rest of the universe. And to get a glimpse—to see how small and insignificant you really are—all one has to do is step outside on a starlit night and look up. We have telescopes of varying degrees, and we can marvel at the moon, the stars, other planets in our solar system, and galaxies beyond. The cosmos are deceptively glorious.

There are worlds beyond this one, and I'm not talking about anything in the trenches of the sea below or the infinite skies above; I'm talking about the dimensions that exist parallel to ours. If there are experts on the subject, I have yet to find them. No amount of research has resulted in a satisfactory explanation for the paranormal events that occurred in the summer of 1999 and what happened recently when I went back to finish the job.

When nightfall came, I made myself a rib eye on the stovetop with a microwaved baked potato and a bottle of Red Stripe. Rarely did I cook for myself, so as a "last meal," this would have to suffice. The clock on the microwave read 8:44 p.m. I still had a few hours to kill before heading to the tunnel. As I looked around the barren kitchen, I thought of Walt and Brandy and wondered what they would think about me living in their old house. I pictured Brandy at the oven, baking blueberry muffins for me and Blake and letting us take turns sampling the uncooked muffin mix because that was the best part.

Walt's study/office, which had always been off-limits to us when we were kids, was just down the hall. I could go in it whenever I wanted to now. I remember Walt sitting in his recliner with his drink, radiating an aura of wanting to be left alone. Knowing the line of work he used to be in made everything click. He didn't hate us, nor was he a miserable workaholic or a hermit. His job demanded decompression. It just so happened that when I would stay the night at their house on the weekends, that was his only time off, and sometimes he worked those hours too. That's probably why we were never allowed in his study, come to think about it. Who knows what kind of gory pictures he had in case files on his desk?

I got up and went up to their bedroom. I struggled to call it my bedroom. Yes, my name was on the deed for the property in Golden Circle, but this wasn't my home. My old house one street over didn't belong to me either. All sentimental value had been robbed from me by the tunnel, by The Recluse. It had taken my family, shattered my childhood, and sowed seeds of hatred for all things remotely related to the neighborhood. I had allowed my memory to be filtered through a traumatized lens full of fear, resentment, and regret.

As I entered the bedroom, I took my last sip of beer and placed the bottle on the dresser. I opened the bottom drawer, took out my only pair of black jeans, and tossed them on the bed before walking to the closet and grabbing a matching black hoodie. There was no doubt that I'd sweat my ass off, but the extra layer of camouflage could make all the difference in the world.

The master bathroom also still felt off-limits to me. I don't think I ever saw it as a kid. Hell, I'd only been in their bedroom once as far as I could remember, and that was to wake Brandy up to take me home because I was seven and staying overnight at their house for the first time, and I needed her to call my mom to come and get me.

I took off my clothes and drew a bath. Baths were never my thing, but still feeling like a man spending his last night on death row, I treated myself to a long, hot soak. Plus, I still had plenty of time before I needed to leave.

The water filled to the top of the tub, and I slowly slid my head under while bending my knees. Initially, the feeling of being submerged relaxed me, in a sensory deprivation type of way, but then I started to think about the tunnel . . . specifically, the black hole that originated between the slats.

I felt myself getting sucked into the darkness, and suddenly the bathwater became that black bile that pumped through the veins of the doppelgängers. It enveloped me and pulled me down to the cold where The Recluse dwelled. I opened my eyes underwater and looked up to see the top of the bathtub a hundred feet above me as I floated in a frozen cave of some hellish landscape. Nothing but darkness surrounded me, but I felt the movement of something massive circling me. I pictured a pale, monstrous creature with tentacles the size of trains dangling from its humanoid body. It opened its eyes, both of them glowing like angler fish luring prey in the ocean depths. The light revealed a mouth of glistening fangs on a gelatinous face that constantly shifted from one victim to the next, like it was showing off all of the people it had collected over the years . . . decades . . . centuries?

Just as it opened its mouth and snapped at me, I sat up in the tub, screaming. I wiped my eyes and looked around the empty bathroom. It knew I was coming. The Recluse saw me driving in the U-Haul. For all I knew, it had some sinister plan cooked up for me, something to drag me out of this world and into its void to do God-knows-what.

I took deep breaths to steady my pulse and leaned back in the tub, making sure to keep my head above water as I rested and waited.

After I got dressed, I walked downstairs and grabbed another beer before heading to the garage. I flipped the light switch and watched the dark room turn white. Totes and brown boxes lined one side of the two-car garage. The Mustang was parked right in front of me. Two orange and white traffic cones with the little reflectors on top were wedged in the reclined passenger seat. I peeked in the back and saw the spike belt and two ROAD CLOSED signs that I'd bought off eBay. Three necessary ingredients to set up a ruse that would hopefully prevent anyone else from getting hurt.

I popped the top off the second beer, took a sip, and opened the trunk. Two bundles of dynamite with the accompanying electric blasting caps and a detonator were tucked away in a black duffel bag, assembled and ready to go. Satisfied, I shut the trunk and kept moving to the other side of the car. I opened the passenger door and then the glove compartment, eyeballing the Glock 19 pistol and the Maglite beside it, just making sure everything was still there.

This was it: the final showdown between me and The Recluse. I saw its grinning face in my mind and shivered. I chugged the rest of the beer and set the bottle on the nearest tote. The alcohol steadied my nerves just enough to keep my mind from convulsing into a full-on panic attack. I looked down and saw the word MOVIES written in black Sharpie on the side of the blue tote.

After all this time, I still had my VHS tapes, plus DVDs, Blu-rays, and 4Ks. Even though every film in my collection was probably available on some streaming service, I'd never gotten out of the habit of buying physical media. I smiled at the thought of the three of us back in the day watching Jean-Claude Van Damme kick ass in my copy of Bloodsport. Just as quickly as that euphoric wave of nostalgia hit, it fled as I remembered Joel shooting Max's doppelgänger, and anger coursed through my veins.

When I got back inside the house, I saw that it was 9:33 p.m. Time inched along. I was getting restless, but I knew that I had to wait. To go too early would put other people in jeopardy. I had to wage this war when everyone else was nestled safely in their beds. And so, I planted myself in the wooden chair at the kitchen table. It was as comfortable as those old desks from high school, so it kept me upright and on edge, where I needed to be. The only time I got up during the following three hours was to piss twice.

At 12:45 a.m., I decided it was time to go. I walked around the first floor of the house one final time, seeing the memories of happier times. I locked the door from the inside and headed to the garage. When I got in the car, I pressed the garage door opener attached to the sun visor and turned on the ignition.

I took the scenic route through Golden Circle—I still can't get used to calling it that—just so I could cruise by Joel and Max's old house. It looked like someone had fixed up the place quite a bit. New siding clung to the front, and they'd remodeled the porch. I kept driving until I approached my childhood home, stopping just in front of it. Whoever lived there now must really love flowers. The porch was hardly visible from the hanging baskets and the potted plants. A meticulous flower bed stretched from the right side of the porch to the corner of the house.

As I stared at the living room window, I tried to focus on the Christmas mornings, the family gatherings, the sleepovers, but my mind kept getting plagued by those frantic days immediately following Max's disappearance. A cold feeling puddled in my gut, and I turned away. This wasn't my home. It was a relic full of ghosts that I wasn't strong enough to visit because the creature responsible still existed, probably relishing its handiwork.

My tour was over. I drove out of Golden Circle, crossing the train tracks that had gotten no less bumpy, then accelerating down the thin black pavement that barely fit two cars. Once I passed all the houses, I knew I had half a mile before the tunnel. There was nothing but a hilly forest on my right and a gradual decline to the river on my left. The tunnel hid behind the curve just ahead of me. I stopped, having arrived at my first stop. I put it in park and got out.

The summer night was muggy, but a cool breeze blew across my face as I ran across the front of the Mustang and opened the passenger door. I bear-hugged one of the traffic cones, heaved it out, and waddled to the rear of the car, stopping in the center of the road. With a slight squat, I lowered it, quietly positioning the deterrent where it would be most effective. I hurried and grabbed one of the ROAD CLOSED signs and placed it beside the cone. It looked convincing enough; I'd believe it if I saw it. But if they didn't see it, I had my backup plan. I reached in and grabbed the police-grade spike belt and dragged it across the road just behind the cone. If some asshole wanted to sneak around, all of their tires would be dismantled. They'd get pissed, not realizing I'd be saving their lives.

Wasting no more time, I ran back to the car and got in the driver's seat. I wiped a gleam of sweat from my brow. Part of that was from lugging the roadwork equipment, no doubt, but the thought of what I had to do next also contributed. I could tell that just by how clammy my palms became. Forcing myself not to think about what could go wrong by driving through the tunnel at night in a red car, I zoomed off.

The entrance appeared as soon as I rounded the curve and passed the FALLING ROCK sign. The lights above the gaping mouth of the tunnel were green, but I would've kept going no matter what color they were. I flipped on my high beams and sped through going sixty miles an hour and counting. The lights inside made my quick dash much less threatening than I'd anticipated.

Once I reached the other side, I thanked God that no other

cars were waiting to come through. It was a lonely road during the day; at night, it was deserted. Still, I didn't slow my pace. As soon as I exited the tunnel, I slammed on the brakes and put the car in park, repeating the same process that I'd just done with the other traffic cone and ROAD CLOSED sign. The only difference this time was that instead of driving off, I went to the passenger side of the car and took out the pistol. I had trained at the range for this moment. Once I was aiming at the red stoplight on the left, I squeezed the trigger and the bulb exploded in a rain of debris. Like a machine, I swung to the right until I had the other light in my sights. Boom! Both lights were out.

The gray electrical box mounted to the roof of the tunnel was my next target. I aimed and fired. My ears rang from the three quick shots. I watched as sparks shot out of the box and the lights that lined the inside of the tunnel strobed their death knell and then turned off. With the gun still in my hand, I got in the car and turned it around so that I faced the tunnel. My gut did that icy thing again as I prepared to drive through, but this time it would be in the darkness.

I kept the high beams on, shifted into first gear, and shot forward. The car's engine roared through the confined space. I gave it as much gas as I could as I passed the slats where The Recluse had reached out and nabbed my best friend. I half-expected a tentacled talon to slither out and jerk the entire car into its hole, but nothing happened. I exited the tunnel unscathed and didn't stop until I was back around the curve, and the entrance was out of sight.

It took me a second to realize how hard I was breathing. I pulled the car onto the one spot on the river side of the road with enough gravel to get most of the vehicle out of the way. I parked and quickly turned it off. There was no time to waste now. I got out and popped the trunk, grabbed the duffel bag and flashlight, and crossed the road. I jumped across the ditch and landed at the start of the path that zigzagged its way up the hilly terrain. Closer to the tunnel was nothing but a straight rock wall, but the farther you got from it, the lower the slope became. This path was how you walked over the tunnel. I'd never taken it myself, but my dad would always point it out to us when we drove by it, educating us on its purpose like it was something he grew up doing.

I booked it up the hill. Aside from a few patches of loose gravel that made me nearly lose my footing, I made it to the top without incident. About fifty yards of a path that cut through the forest separated me from standing on top of the tunnel. Trees surrounded me like gargantuan spectators from an ancient time, and with their roots firmly embedded in this cursed soil, it wouldn't surprise me if one of them reached out and snatched my ankle, holding me upside down until The Recluse could come to collect its next meal.

But my target wasn't the tunnel. Well, that came next. I stopped when I reached the massive boulder that protruded over the entrance to the tunnel like a balcony with a perfect view of Hell. The rock that I stood on had been threatening to come tumbling down on unsuspecting cars since I was a little kid. I looked around and decided that this was as good a spot as any. I unzipped the bag, carefully removed one bundle of dynamite, and assembled the electronic blasting cap. The remote screen lit up when I powered it on. As instructed, I synced the blasting cap to the remote so that all I had to do was press the button and kaboom!

I crept back to the edge of the "falling rock" and looked down at the dark tunnel. No sign of The Recluse. That was good; it meant every theory I had about its ability to enter our world via the color red was true. I'd driven by the slats, but it was too quick for any portal to its world to open fast enough for it to emerge. But now it was time for The Recluse to come out of hiding. If it wanted in our world so bad, I would gladly open the door for it.

Running even faster down the hill, I nearly busted my ass on the loose gravel again, but I regained my composure. Twisting an ankle and falling down to the road would have definitely been a hindrance to my plan. When I reached the bottom, I hopped the ditch and ran back across the road to the car. I nearly shit when I saw headlights approaching from the road to Golden Circle. I crouched and watched a truck slow down when it got to my sign. It sat there idling for a few seconds.

"Go, goddamnit," I said.

The truck slowly backed up and turned around. My heart rate returned to normal. I opened the trunk and placed the duffel bag back inside. Just like the procedure I'd performed on the hill, I assembled the explosive and synced it to my remote. My screen now said CHARGE 1 and CHARGE 2.

"Charge 2 is the car," I said to myself, knowing it would be a colossal fuckup of cosmic proportions if I pressed the wrong button at the wrong time. I shut the trunk and got back in the car. After taking a moment to breathe and picture every part of the plan going exactly as I'd envisioned it, I started the Mustang and crept toward the tunnel. There would be no mad dash this time. I wanted the bastard to come out.

I passed the FALLING ROCK sign and nodded my head at it like it was a knowing accomplice. My windows squeaked when I rolled them down. No music came from the speakers. Other than the chirping crickets and an occasional tree frog, it was eerily silent. The gaping maw of the tunnel grew the closer I got to it.

I stopped just short of the entrance and turned off my headlights. I sat there as my pulse quickened. I felt like I was in a rowboat floating atop a bottomless ocean as an open mouth swam up from below me. All I could do was wait and keep my ears open.

"Maaavvverickkkk," a devilish voice from inside the tunnel said.

My already heightened senses turned hypervigilant. I listened to dragging footsteps come from the darkness, getting louder as they got closer. That's when I saw the shape of a body as tall as the tunnel lumber into the moonlight.

It took all of my willpower not to soil myself as I stared at the disfigured body standing before me. It was over twenty feet tall and had to crane its neck to avoid hitting the roof of the tunnel. Long strands of hair—no, tentacles—dangled from its head and face, curling and twisting down its elongated abdomen. Its crooked arms stretched all the way to its ankles like a primate about to run on all fours.

This was the creature that had destroyed my life. An abomination that had somehow found a loophole through the very threshold of time and space to terrorize this insignificant part of the world.

Why? It didn't make sense, the randomness of it all. But then again, the universe is a hostile place; we just managed to hit the cosmic lottery and exist on a planet that supports and nourishes life.

I grabbed the detonator and put it in the cupholder just as I shifted into first gear and drove straight toward it. An animalistic screech came from the beast. I flicked on my lights and high beams and saw The Recluse in all its grotesque glory. Two vertical eyelids closed over its black, sharklike eyeballs.

"Get blinded, bitch." I shifted again and floored the gas

pedal. I screamed like a warrior running across the battlefield and didn't stop until I drilled The Recluse with the Mustang. Its massive body folded over, denting the roof of the Mustang so badly that it nearly hit my head. The car shook like it was driving over speed bumps, and I realized its legs were caught underneath.

I grabbed the detonator from the cupholder and kept the car aimed at the widening black hole growing amongst the slats like I did the last time we encountered one another. An immediate shadow covered the car from front to back, and suddenly everything was dark and cold. At first, I felt like I was falling, but in a matter of seconds, we were floating. I was in the dark place, the cold black hole that had claimed my family and friends. I thought back to Max calling me on the walkie-talkie the night he got pulled in there and how terrified he must've been.

My headlights weren't working. I felt like I was at the bottom of the Mariana Trench—the deepest part of the ocean. All of a sudden, the car shook violently as The Recluse released its grasp and disappeared into the abyss. I looked through every window, frantically searching for the doorway back to my world that I knew was rapidly closing. The red car was inside. I'd willingly driven it in there. Terror hit me at that realization. I had willingly entered the tunnel. I don't know why I didn't think of that one specific ramification of my actions: I could become a doppelgänger.

The back window shattered and suddenly the inside of the car was below freezing. I clutched the gun and the detonator, but before I could turn around to see what happened, a tentacle shot through the passenger window, past my face, and burst through my window. I looked to my right and saw The Recluse floating outside the car like some kind of ghostly apparition. Now that my eyes had adjusted to the dark, I could see that this was no endless void at all. We were inside a cave of some sort.

A black gelatinous wall behind The Recluse stretched as far up and down as I could see. Before I could survey my surroundings further, the snarling monster jerked the car toward its open mouth, a mouth that was stretching like a serpent waiting to devour a large meal. Its metallic fangs reflected light, and I felt a glimmer of hope in realizing that the portal was still open somewhere—as that was the only light source I knew of—so I could still get out.

When I moved toward my open window, I detected no gravity in this world. I let go of the gun and watched it float out of my window as The Recluse pulled the Mustang closer. Still holding the detonator, I grabbed the side of the broken window without thinking and buried a shard of glass into the meat of my right palm. The adrenaline numbed the pain as I still managed to propel myself through the open window.

Floating freely in this frozen, forgotten world, I felt like an astronaut adrift in space. I saw more of The Recluse's lair from this vantage point. The black walls rippled, and I recognized the substance as the same ooze that had come out of every doppelgänger I'd encountered. We were inside of a sphere, and we weren't alone. A shiver shot down my spine when I noticed all the faces trapped in the walls—frozen and lifeless like they'd been held captive, drained of their likeness, and spat out as clones.

I looked up—if there was an "up" in this place—and saw the shrinking window that led to the tunnel. This was the same image I'd prophesized in the bathtub: me, trapped in the darkness, desperately trying to make it to the light. Below, The Recluse had pulled the Mustang into its hideously gaping mouth and started to swallow it, trunk first. It looked like one of those videos of an anaconda swallowing a cow whole. It hadn't noticed I had fled yet.

And for one brief moment, I felt pity for the being, whatever it was—alien, demon, ghost—it didn't matter. This creature, trapped in this frozen prison, all alone in the darkness, forced to catch glimpses of humans living freely in a world much more appealing than its own, yet it was bound here. Its only reprieve was through abducting and mimicking the people it so bitterly envied. The Recluse wanted to get as much of itself into our world as it could. That's why it kept trying to lure more willing victims into its web. It was lonely.

A crunching noise reverberated throughout the cave. I looked down and saw that The Recluse had fully swallowed the car. Its eyes locked on mine, and I could see the rage in the contorting look on its face. Though still humanoid in shape, it had grown to the size of a giant squid. I could see its limbs bracing to make a lunge for me, and I knew it was almost time.

Twenty feet separated me from the hole in the slats, and about the same distance between me and The Recluse. I made swimming motions to try and cover as much ground as I could before that thing launched at me. I felt the rumbling in the atmosphere as the liquid walls rippled. An explosion of force shook the cave, and I knew the beast had taken off like a rocket ship.

Ten feet was left until freedom, but I knew I wouldn't make it. The time had come for the first blast. I looked down at the detonator in my hand. I saw an open mouth approaching, and I froze in terror. Only by pure instinct, my thumb pressed the button.

A ring around The Recluse's distended torso exploded outward. The cave lit up, temporarily blinding me and rocketing me forward like I'd been thrown from a motorcycle. I tried to keep my eyes open and thanked God as I shot through the closing portal. I landed with a thud on the hard pavement in the tunnel, rolling across the road and smacking back-first against the wooden slats.

My eyes shot open as I watched the severed torso of The Recluse shoot through the portal just as it closed for the last time. I quickly scooted out of the way as the pale figure shrieked and flew across the road exactly like I did. Its head cracked against the edge of one of the slats like a wedge splitting a coconut. I slowly got to my feet in the dark tunnel and eyeballed the thing, which had shrunk considerably in size. Its tentacles had retracted into its body like a salted slug. This once ferocious Lovecraftian nightmare just lay on the ground, reduced to nothing but a pale alien humanoid that had been blown apart from the waist down.

A pond of that black substance had already formed where its legs used to be, and a smaller puddle grew from its leaking skull. It faced away from me, toward the tunnel's exit back to Golden Circle. I cursed myself for not snagging my gun, but only James Bond or John Wick could've pulled off that maneuver.

The monster lay still. I finally worked up the nerve to take steps toward the body. A pungent odor like rotten fish hit me in the face as I got closer. I tried to breathe only through my mouth, but it was damn near impossible. When I was about three feet away from it, I stopped.

"Hey," I said.

Its body twitched just enough to make me think it could've been a trick of the eye, but I knew better.

"Hey, you piece of shit. I know you're still alive. You wanted me back here. Well, here I am."

A sickening snap sounded as its head spun around to face mine. Its eyes and mouth were wide open, and it shook like a person in the late stages of Parkinson's disease. The look on its face was one of fear. This creature that had destroyed my life and plagued my dreams was scared of me. It knew it was about to die. I wondered if it even knew that it could die or even how it came to be in the first place.

But then its expression changed. Its brow relaxed, and a Grinch-like smile curled up its face. Its arms snapped into perfect right angles as it lifted itself off the road. I should've known better. It was dying, sure, but that didn't mean it couldn't take me with it. My mouth dropped as I watched the dangling flaps of its torn torso fold up and seal together like modeling clay. Of course it could do that. This was a being that mimicked and replicated. It could change form at will, and I was an idiot for underestimating it.

I had to get out of there, but I couldn't go toward town. I needed to get past that bastard, back on the Golden Circle side. It forced me into action when it skittered across the road on its arms, laughing with glee at the effect it still had over me. And that would be its downfall. I played up being terrified and even stumbled backward like I didn't know what to do. Just as it leaped off the road at me like a face hugger from the Alien movies, I ducked underneath it and sprinted toward the exit.

The Recluse growled behind me, obviously pissed off, but I was too far ahead of it now.

I ran into the moonlight and kept running, not looking back until I approached the FALLING ROCK sign.

"Maaaavvvvverricckkk..."

The hairs on the back of my neck prickled as I turned around.

The Recluse hung from the top of the tunnel like a spider

and flung itself off, flipping through the air and landing on the road. It crawled toward me like some kind of wolf approaching its wounded prey . . . just like I hoped it would.

I raised the detonator.

It stopped and cocked its head.

"This is for Max."

I pressed the button for the second charge. The dynamite wedged in the hillside exploded with a bang and a cloud of dust as the massive boulder that took up most of the ridge near the tunnel's entrance finally broke free. A chunk of solid rock the size of a school bus barreled down the rocky terrain. I looked at The Recluse, and it looked at me. A knowing grin spread across its jagged teeth a second before being flattened completely.

I watched as the boulder continued its forward momentum into the corner of the tunnel, decimating the left side. And that was all it took for the domino effect to occur. Once the front fell, the interior slats on that side snapped like a busted rib cage as the mountain caved in on itself. It wasn't enough to completely level the tunnel, but the area that housed the portal to The Recluse's cave was no more.

I allowed myself only a few seconds to savor the victory. This place would soon be flooded with first responders of every sort. As sirens called in the distance, I turned around and started to jog back to Golden Circle, pushing myself beyond the threshold of exhaustion until I hit the train tracks.

As evidenced by this final entry, I survived, and I got away with it. Five weeks have passed, and the authorities have no leads on the bombing of the tunnel. Or if they do, they're not sharing them with the press. I no longer live in Blake's old house in Golden Circle. I listed it last week and took the first offer. They lowballed me, but I didn't care. We're supposed to close on it next month.

I moved down south to an apartment in Orlando. I figured it best to get out of Dodge just in case, plus I'd be closer to Jill. She actually called me when she heard about the explosion of the tunnel that led to our childhood home and asked if I'd heard about it. I said I hadn't. I waited for her response, and she let me know how glad she was that it had happened. She even pressed me to come visit her and her family. I told her I'd be happy to and that I'd actually be working remotely in Florida for a while. I figured I'd been in the dark too long. Sunshine and family would hopefully expedite the trauma I still carried.

But things have only gotten worse since the last night at the tunnel. The initial relief I had has once again morphed into paranoia and an insidious notion over which I can't stop obsessing.

It started getting bad again at night. I would lay there and wonder if part of The Recluse had somehow gotten inside of me. My dreams are once again plagued by memories of being in that cave in the tunnel, floating in the absolute darkness, surrounded by the bodies—the victims—of all the poor souls that monster had absorbed and masqueraded as.

Now, it's to the point where just closing my eyes for more than a few seconds transports me back to that sad, desolate Hell. A few times I've felt the freezing and floating sensation, and I'm convinced that I'm still there—that I never left the cave, and this has all been a delusion replaying in my static body that's in an eternal state of stasis with Jill, Max, Blake, Joel, Darla, Walt, Brandy, Sheriff Potts, and the countless others.

There was a reason I was compelled to go back to the tunnel after all those years. Was that it? Had I been duped? What if the real me is still there, and I'm just seeing the world through the eyes of my doppelgänger? Or did I really kill The Recluse and put a dead end to its tunnel into our world? As the sleepless nights add up, I honestly don't know the answer to that question.

What I do know is that when I look in the mirror, I see my face. It's no longer the carefree thirteen-year-old boy who played with his best friends during the summer of 1999, who had parents who discussed the Y2K hysteria and sisters who played together and secretly made me jealous; my reflection is there. It's only when I stare too long that I notice the darkness in my pupils, and the longer I look, the more I see the abyss between the slats staring back at me.

THE END

Acknowledgments

Thank you to my family for always supporting my writing. I wrote this novella while editing Mean Spirited and writing The Exorcist's House: Genesis, so I wasn't always the most pleasant person to be around. My wife and children have my infinite gratitude for putting up with my bouts of brooding and anxiety and being the anchors keeping me grounded.

This is a personal tale that borrows heavily from my own experiences. The characters and settings represented are amalgamations of childhood friends and locations. Thank you to the Riverbend crew of goofy kids who participated in the magic of my childhood before the paths of life led us in different directions. We'll always have the trains, the tunnel, and the memories.

I must also thank my Patreon subscribers. This story began as a serialized novella, exclusive to Patrons of a certain tier. I had no blueprint or professional editor as I cranked out monthly installments. This was both exhilarating and terrifying. My process as a "pantser" is to write my first draft and then go back and make it look like I knew what I was doing all along. The Patreon version of Dead End Tunnel exposed my strengths and weaknesses and left me feeling naked at times. However, the readers responded to the narrative and motivated me to work harder and tie it all together. Thank you to the following champions of my writing endeavors:

Rebecca Rogers
Daniel Hilden
Lisa Breanne
Meredith Foster
Abby Farmer
Anett Ashton
Ashley Chmielewski
Brandon Wilson
Brittany Powers
Francesca Catalano
Darrin Hall
Jennifer Whitney
Joe Bridwell
Joseph Miller
Liz Wallace
Malina Roos
Missy Johnson
Montez Oudenaarden
Shannon Roberts
Teresa Howell
Amanda Ruzsa
Amy Porter
April Haas
Camille Sara
Damaris Quinones
Kelly Jobes
Kristina Lee
Lara Watkins
Linda McIntire
Makayla Martin
Mari Pittelman
Mary Sepko
Alexia Ashford
Molly Mix
Nancy Elizabeth
Rebecca Cavanaugh
Roger Geis
Ryan Gairdner

Samantha Noseworthy
Sara Dougherty
Sean Dicristofaro
Sophia McIntyre
Stephen Bailey
Trudy Meiser
Candy Mosley
Cassidy Budke
Jess Norris
Rae Moore
Alicia Toothman
Ashley Mohler
Brenda Franks
Carrie Hibbard
Catherine Miley
Dalanna Bottorff
Debbie Thornton
Dustin Blechschmidt
Gage Greenwood
Georgia Kolster
Indiana Knight
Jay Bower
Jenn Osborn
John Durgin
Joseph Murnane
Kara Mulholland
Mary Trujillo
Michelle Edwards
Mike Hughes
Missy Bentley
Monique Beasley
Robin Moore
Robin Spear
Sam Cox
Stacy Grimes
Trina Thompson
Ugur Kutay

www.ingramcontent.com/pod-product-compliance
Ingram Content Group UK Ltd.
Pitfield, Milton Keynes, MK11 3LW, UK
UKHW020958070525
5798UKWH00024B/225

9 798218 437138